TH
TO
CENTRAL ACADEMY . . .

*Discover the chilling adventures that
shadow the halls and stalk the students of*
TERROR ACADEMY!

LIGHTS OUT

Mandy Roberts digs up the
suspicious past of the new assistant principal.
The man her widowed mother plans to marry . . .

STALKER

A tough punk comes back to Central with one
requirement to complete: vengeance . . .

SIXTEEN CANDLES

Kelly Langdon discovers there's more to being
popular than she thought—like staying alive . . .

SPRING BREAK

It's the vacation from hell.
And it's up to Laura Hollister to save her family.
And herself . . .

THE NEW KID

There's something about the new transfer student.
He's got a deadly secret . . .

STUDENT BODY

No one's safe at Central—
when a killer roams the halls . . .

continued . . .

NIGHT SCHOOL

The most handsome teacher in school . . .
is a vampire!

SCIENCE PROJECT

There's a new formula for terror:
E = mc scared . . .

THE PROM

It's a party that could raise the dead . . .

THE IN CROWD

A group of misfits learn a deadly lesson:
if you don't fit in, you may be out
—for good!

SUMMER SCHOOL

Making up is hard to do —
when terror is waiting at summer school . . .

BREAKING UP

When rich girl meets greaser boy,
love can be a real killer . . .

THE SUBSTITUTE

Her name is Ms. Green.
And her assignments are murder . . .

SCHOOL SPIRIT

Are the Central Academy Wildcats sore losers?
Or vicious killers?

TERROR ACADEMY

BOY CRAZY

NICHOLAS PINE

B

BERKLEY BOOKS, NEW YORK

For Little Monkey D

BOY CRAZY

A Berkley Book / published by arrangement with
the author

PRINTING HISTORY
Berkley edition / May 1995

ISBN: 0-425-14727-4

BERKLEY®
Berkley Books are published by The Berkley Publishing Group,
200 Madison Avenue, New York, New York 10016.
BERKLEY and the "B" design
are trademarks belonging to Berkley Publishing Corporation.

PRINTED IN THE UNITED STATES OF AMERICA

10 9 8 7 6 5 4 3

ONE

Shannon Riley sighed and lifted her crystal green eyes to the tinted window of the bus. The motorcoach sped south toward Shannon's new home. She peered out at the deep hues of summer, wondering what Port City would be like once she actually arrived there. Her father's letters had described the small New England town in glowing terms. But Shannon's hopes weren't high because she knew her father had a tendency to exaggerate.

"Shannon, I'm thirsty."

Shannon turned to glare at Patrick Riley, her bothersome fourteen-year-old brother. "Don't whine, Patrick."

"I'm not whining!"

Shannon shook her head. "Honestly, you can be such a wimp sometimes."

1

"You're hogging all the water in your backpack!" he challenged. "I need a drink before my mouth catches on fire."

Shannon motioned to the luggage rack above them. "Get my pack and I'll give you some water."

Patrick slid out of the seat, which was at the dead rear of the bus, the last row. Shannon worried about Patrick. He was a smart kid, having been skipped a grade in grammar school. Patrick usually stood a head shorter than most of the older boys in his class. And his incredible intelligence often set him apart from everyone else, even the older kids.

Patrick dropped down into the seat, shuffling the backpack to his sister. His eyes were as green as Shannon's, his hair a light auburn color. Patrick took after their mother, who had died last year at the end of a long, debilitating disease.

Shannon shuddered as she handed the water bottle to her brother. "Don't drink it all. I don't have any money left."

Patrick took a short sip from the bottle and gave it back to her. "I wish we were staying at Grammie's," he offered in a disgusted tone. "I liked it in Maine. I liked living out in the woods too."

So did I, Shannon thought.

Patrick folded his arms over his chest.

"Dad's just jerking us around with this job of his. He's pumping it up, but I know it's all a daydream."

Shannon felt the same way, but she wasn't going to trash her father. "Dad's doing a lot better, Patrick. Mom . . ." Her voice cracked for a moment. "It was hard on him."

Patrick gave her a hostile look. "It was hard on me too! But I didn't drink myself into a looney bin!"

"Lower your voice," Shannon snapped.

He looked away. "It's true, Shannon!"

"It's a disease," she told him. "Alcoholics can't help it, Patrick. Dad is recovering now. And he needs us. We can't let him down."

"Yeah, right."

Patrick began to sulk, closing his eyes and pretending to go to sleep.

Shannon put the bottle of water back into her knapsack and stuffed the pack under the seat. For a moment, she felt bad about fighting with her brother. They were both scared, heading for a new town, a new life. Jack Riley, their father, was boasting of a great job at the Port City Shipyard. And it was possible. After all, he had been to college to study engineering, earning a degree. Things had been fine at his other job, too, until her mother was diagnosed with cancer. It had all happened so quickly, so horribly.

Gazing toward the window again, Shannon caught a glimpse of her own reflection in the glass. The dark hair came from her father's side of the family. She had let the brown tresses grow long during the summer. Maybe she would get her hair cut in Port City.

She studied her tanned face. There had been a time in her life when Shannon was one of the most popular kids in her school. Her wholesome looks and vibrant personality had attracted a lot of boys, even a couple of steadies. Everything had changed after the death of her mother.

Shannon still had dreams about the horrible times that had followed the funeral. Her father's descent into madness had taken a classic toll—denial, anger, grief, and acceptance. They hadn't really seen him since he had been released from the treatment center. Now they had to face him with all the terrible memories that refused to leave their heads.

The birthday party, she thought. He had acted like such a jerk. Her friends had all been mortified. None of them would even write to her after she left Manchester. They thought he was a pervert.

There was so much to think about, to

worry about. A new school. A new town.
She wouldn't be anyone, just the new kid.
What would they do to her? How would
they treat her? She hated having to spend
her junior year at a different school. And
what about her senior year? She had already ordered her class ring from
Manchester High. Would they give her the
deposit back?

A wave of anxiety rolled through Shannon, putting her on the edge of her seat.
What if everything turned to garbage in
Port City, the way it had after her mother's
death? Shannon wasn't sure she could take
that again. The summer at her grandmother's place in Maine had helped, but deep
inside, Shannon knew she had not re-
gained her full strength.

"Shannon?" Patrick had opened one eye.

"What?" she snapped at him.

He sighed. "I'm sorry about what I said.
About Dad, I mean. I—I was just upset.
And I'm a little scared."

"Just a little?" Shannon replied. "I'm
petrified. But we have to give it a chance."

Patrick scoffed and looked out the window. "A new school. New bullies to kick my
butt."

"Maybe it won't be like that," she offered.

"I wonder where we're gonna live,"
Patrick said blankly.

I just exist since Mom died, Shannon thought. I don't *live*.

She remembered how she had handled all the household bills when her father began his bouts of drinking. It had been rough, dodging the bill collectors, trying to get her father's paycheck before he cashed it at the liquor store. Shannon had almost broken down from the strain.

How can I believe that everything will be all right?

The bus rolled past a sign stating that Port City was a mere sixty miles away. They had left her grandmother's house at six o'clock in the morning. And the bus had been a local until it reached Lewiston. The ride had seemingly taken forever, but now it looked like they were going to arrive in Port City around three o'clock on this sunny August day.

"Are you okay?" Patrick asked.

She nodded. "Yeah, I'm fine."

"You look weird," he said.

Shannon grimaced. "Thanks a lot."

"No, I just mean—"

"I know what you mean, Patrick. Just—"

Shannon stopped when she realized that someone was standing in front of her. Patrick also turned to look at the hulking figure that had appeared from one of the other seats. It was the fat, greasy-haired man who had gotten on the bus in Lewiston. He had staggered down the aisle to collapse into a snoring slumber that had gradually become shallow breathing.

"Whoa," Patrick muttered.

Shannon's eyes narrowed. "What do you want?"

The man waved a cigarette in front of her. "Can only smoke in the last three rows. Gotta have a smoke."

Shannon could smell the alcoholic stench on him. She recognized the odor from experience. They had to get away from him. He reminded Shannon of the way her father had been.

"Hey, you got a match?" the man asked.

Shannon shook her head. "No, but we'll move. Come on, Patrick. Let's find another seat. The bus is practically empty, so we won't have any trouble."

Patrick started to get up. "Sure, Sis."

The greasy man pushed him back into the seat. "Don't have to move."

Shannon glared at him. "Get out of our way."

The man smiled. "Hey, you ain't bad. Kinda cute."

He's going to do something stupid, just like my father at my sixteenth birthday party.

"Scoot over so I can siddown, kids."

Shannon shook her head again. "No, you get out of the way. We'll let you have these seats."

He reached out toward Shannon.

Just like my drunken father.

"Pretty girl. Tell the kid here to get lost. You'n me can party. Look what I got."

Reaching into his sweat-stained jacket, the man produced a half-empty pint of cheap whiskey.

"Leave us alone!" Patrick cried.

The man drew back his hand to cuff Shannon's younger brother. But the mechanical voice froze him. It boomed out of the speaker above the driver.

"What's going on back there?" the driver said into his microphone.

"None of your business," the greasy man snapped over his shoulder. "Just keep driving."

"He's bothering us!" Patrick cried. "He won't let us move to another seat!"

"Shut up, you little—"

The driver's voice filled the coach. "Move away from those kids right now!"

The intruder wheeled to point his finger at the driver. "I thought I told you to—"

Suddenly the bus swerved into the emergency lane of the interstate highway.

The drunken man fell backward, sprawling in the aisle as the bus came to a halt.

Before the sot could regain his feet, the driver was on him, lifting him from the floor.

"I didn't want you on the bus when they let you board in Lewiston," the driver said. "I hate drunks."

He dragged the protesting man down the aisle and promptly tossed him from the front door of the bus. The man banged on the door but he couldn't get back in. The driver walked toward Shannon and her brother, smiling at them.

"Thank you," Shannon said.

Patrick nodded. "Yeah, thanks."

"Your grandmother asked me to watch out for you," he told them. "I'm sorry about that guy."

"Yeah, me too!" Patrick offered.

Shannon tried to smile back, though she was trembling all over. "Thank you again."

"You're going to Port City, right?" the driver asked.

"Yes," Shannon replied.

He winked at her. "You're gonna love Port City. It's a great little town."

I hope so, Shannon thought.

The driver returned to the wheel, guiding the bus back onto the interstate, leaving the drunk behind.

Just like Dad, she said to herself.

She winced at the image of Jack Riley trying to kiss her best friend at the sweet sixteen party.

He had been drunk then.

Maybe it would be different.

Maybe she could get her life back.

The old life, when everything had been nice and Shannon Riley had been happy.

Maybe.

TWO

Shannon's eyes grew wide when the roof-tops of Port City rose in the distance. She had a glorious view of the quaint New England village from atop a high bridge that spanned the Tide Gate River. Port City shimmered under the warm light of late summer. For a moment, Shannon and Patrick were filled with a fresh sense of hope.

"Wow," Patrick muttered. "It's cool. This is where we're going to live?"

Shannon nodded as they passed the sign that read, WELCOME TO PORT CITY. She gazed down the channel of the Tide Gate River, spying the shipyard in the distance. Maybe her father had actually found a decent job in this place.

The bus took an off ramp, leaving the

interstate to navigate the narrow streets of the downtown area. Shannon took in the red brick structures that surrounded Market Square. There were cute shops and quaint storefronts along the sidewalks of the square. A high, white steeple rose from North Church. Church bells sounded the hour—three o'clock—as the bus rolled to a halt in front of the station.

"Port City," the driver said over the loud-speaker.

Shannon reached under the seat for her pack. "This is it, little brother."

Patrick squinted at the sidewalk out-side. "I don't see Dad anywhere. What if—"

"Let's just go," Shannon replied.

And pray he's sober! she added to herself.

They left their seats, stepping down the aisle.

The driver smiled as they passed him. "Good luck, kids."

"Thanks," Shannon replied.

She came off the bus first, looking for their father.

Patrick was right behind her. "I don't see him yet, Shannon. I bet he's—"

"Don't say it," Shannon warned.

"Hey, I—"

She pushed him. "Just shut up, Patrick!"

Her brother was about to utter a hostile

reply when the man's voice rose from the station.

"Shannon! Patrick! Over here!"

A tall, slender man came toward them. He wore a white tennis shirt, khaki trousers, and new running shoes. At first, Shannon didn't recognize her own father. But when he took off the dark glasses that covered half his face, she could see the twinkling green eyes that she and Patrick had inherited from him.

"Wow," Patrick offered in a whisper. "He looks great."

Shannon couldn't believe the transformation. The grizzle-faced drunk was gone. Her father smiled again, the way he had before their mother died. His eyes were glowing, his face lifted in a pleasant expression.

Careful, she told herself. Don't get taken in just yet.

He could backslide.

Jack Riley ran to his children, embracing them. He had tears in his eyes. Shannon was crying as well.

"I missed you guys so much," he said in a faltering voice. "I'm so glad to see you."

Shannon wiped the tears from her cheeks. "We're glad to see you too, Dad."

Patrick, who was fighting back his own

tears, shook his head in disgust. "Stop crying, you two."

Mr. Riley gestured toward the parking area. "Come on, before I have to feed the meter again."

"We have to get our bags," Shannon told him. "They're in the luggage compartment."

The driver smiled at Shannon as they retrieved their baggage. Almost everything that Shannon and Patrick owned had been stuffed into four suitcases, a duffle bag, and a small trunk. They lugged it to a small, red Subaru station wagon that wore quite a bit of rust on the body.

Mr. Riley laughed a little. "It's not much to look at," he offered in an apologetic tone, "but it's paid for and it runs. It should do us until we can get something better."

"It's fine," Shannon said.

Patrick nodded. "Yeah, it's okay."

"It has four-wheel drive," Mr. Riley went on. "It'll be great for the winter."

Shannon put her hand on his shoulder. "Really, Dad. It's fine. Let's load everything."

There were able to put all their luggage in the back of the small wagon.

"Shotgun!" Patrick called. "I get to sit in the front seat with Dad!"

"Go ahead," Shannon told him. "I don't care."

"Come on," Mr. Riley said. "I want you kids to see your new home. Oh, it's great to be with you."

They piled into the Subaru with Patrick claiming the front seat. Shannon didn't mind sitting in back. She wanted to keep watching her father, to see if there were any signs of the demon who had all but ruined her previous life.

He seems so happy, she thought.

She could almost hear her mother's sweet voice.

You have to forgive him, Shannon.

I know, Mom.

He didn't know what he was doing, Shannon.

"I know," she said aloud, answering the inner voice.

Her father's green eyes flashed in the rearview mirror. "What, Shannon?"

She tried to smile. "Uh, I know I like this place already, Dad. It's so nice."

She could see his grinning reflection in the mirror. "Kids, it's great to see you. Things are going to be different this time. I promise."

Patrick didn't reply. Nor did Shannon. They had both heard his empty promises before. It was hard for them to be hopeful with everything that had happened after their mother's death.

"I've got a really good job at the shipyard," Mr. Riley went on. "I'm only a draftsman now, but they're starting me at twenty thousand a year. Once I'm in the company, I'll have a chance at a position in the engineering department. We're going to have a fresh start in Port City, kids. I swear."

The Subaru left Market Square to head east on Middle Road. Shannon gazed out the window, thinking that Port City was one of the most beautiful places she had ever seen. They passed a large, green area called Fair Common Park. The place was alive with picnickers and cute boys throwing Frisbees.

"Can we go to this park?" Patrick asked.

"Sure," his father replied. "Hey, would you two like to see where you'll be going to school?"

Shannon sat up straight in the backseat, leaning over to peek between the bucket seats. "Take us there. Please! I'd love to see the new school, Dad."

"No problem," he replied cheerfully.

Shannon leaned back. He *did* seem more like his old self. What if her father had really returned? The nice guy, the solid rock that she had counted on for the first fifteen years of her young life.

Mr. Riley turned onto a side street called Rockbury Lane. As they neared the end of the narrow avenue, the buildings of Central Academy became more apparent. Patrick's mouth fell open as he counted the red brick structures on a campus that must've spanned three city blocks.

"Six buildings, and all of them huge!" Patrick said.

Mr. Riley nodded as he pulled the car to the curb. "That's the gym. You can see the edge of the football stadium there. See it, just beyond the pool dome."

Shannon smiled. "It has a pool?"

"Uh-huh. And that's the cafeteria, the three classroom buildings, and a library. They call it Central Academy."

Patrick shook his head. "It's like some fancy prep school or something, Dad."

"They have a great science department too," Mr. Riley replied. "I know you've always been good at science, Patrick."

Shannon gazed at the campus, thinking that for once she agreed with Patrick. Central Academy did look like a fancy prep school. How could her father afford to send them to this place?

"Dad, we can go to a public school," Shannon offered. "You can't afford—"

"Central Academy *is* a public school, Shannon. It's one of the top-rated schools in the northeast. And you're lucky enough to be going there."

The words formed on her lips. "Central Academy."

"I think I'm going to like it here," Patrick said.

Mr. Riley looked over his shoulder at his daughter in the backseat. "Shannon, you're finally going to get your driver's license, so you can help me with shopping and stuff like that."

Shannon's face beamed with newfound pride. "Really?"

"Sure. Hey, I have to make a couple of stops. You guys want to come along?"

"Sure," Patrick replied.

Shannon nodded her approval. She wanted to see more of the pretty little town. Her eyes lingered for a moment on the sturdy walls of Central Academy.

It seemed like a great school.

On the outside.

Dad always exaggerates, she thought.

If he said he was making twenty thousand, he was probably making fifteen or sixteen thousand a year at his job.

If he said the car was paid for, it had probably come from a sleazy "Buy Here,

Pay Here" lot that would soak him for payments.

Shannon had to keep her head about her. Her father was a dreamer who sometimes forgot the details. Jack Riley had imagination and talent, but he often neglected to pay heed to common sense. It had gotten the family into trouble before.

The Subaru returned to Middle Road, bearing now for Tremont Mall on the other side of Port City.

As they passed a graveyard known as Old Cemetery, Patrick grimaced and said, "Dead people."

"Quite a few famous dead people buried in there," Mr. Riley told them. "They say the ghosts rise up at night to ride the winds from the river."

Patrick chortled. "Yeah, right, Dad. I'm too old for that stuff now."

Shannon gave a shudder, remembering her mother's funeral. Sometimes she thought her mother was living inside her. That little voice resonated in her brain, giving advice, chiding, directing, blaming. The voice kept telling Shannon to forgive her father for the things he had done.

My own voice tells me to be careful, she thought.

Forgive him.

Shannon shook her head, trying to clear the cobwebs.

This was a new start.

She had to believe in herself, in her family.

But when they approached Tremont Mall, Shannon saw the sign and the arrow pointing the direction to the state liquor store.

She tensed in the backseat.

Mr. Riley turned into the parking lot, following the sign.

He's going to do it, Shannon thought. *He's going to get drunk and ruin my life again.*

No new town.

No fresh start.

Just another stage for the old nightmare to tread.

THREE

Patrick turned to stare at his sister over the top of the seat. He had seen the liquor store sign as well. A stunned, wide-eyed expression had frozen his countenance. He didn't want to relive the nightmare either.

The car drew closer to the line of storefronts. Mr. Riley continued to babble about Port City, trying to sell his children on the merits of the quaint seacoast town. But Shannon and Patrick weren't listening. They just stared at the liquor store as Mr. Riley steered the car into a parking space.

"Come on, kids," he told them. "Let's go."

He wanted them to come into the liquor store with him!

Shannon leaned forward. "Dad—"

But he was already out of the car, slamming the door.

Patrick mouthed the words, "What are we going to do?"

"Try to stop him," Shannon replied.

She jumped out of the Subaru, running after her father. "Dad, don't, please!" She grabbed his shoulder and turned him toward her.

Mr. Riley frowned. "What is it?"

Shannon nodded toward the front window of the liquor store. "Don't go in there. Please. Just don't."

Mr. Riley stepped back. "Go in where?"

"Dad—"

Patrick ran up beside her. "Don't do it, Dad. Don't freakin' do it!"

Mr. Riley glanced over his shoulder. "What're you talking about, kids? I—"

His eyes fell on the window of the liquor store. "Oh, I see. I understand."

Shannon grimaced, thinking that he was going to get violent. He had been crazy before, freaking out if they tried to stop him from buying alcohol. But when he turned to face them again, tears streamed from his eyes.

Mr. Riley held out his arms. "Kids, come here. Come on!"

Reluctantly, they hugged him.

"It's not like that anymore," he told them. "I'm not heading to buy booze. I'm going to The Shopping Basket. See, right next to the liquor store."

Shannon had begun to cry. "I'm sorry, Dad, it's just . . ."

He stroked her hair as she clung tightly to him. "It's not like that anymore. Okay?"

Patrick wiped his wet face with the back of his hand. "Okay, Dad. Let go of me!"

He drew back, sniffling.

Mr. Riley laughed. "Yeah, I didn't like to hug my father either when I was fourteen."

Shannon sighed, releasing herself from the embrace. "Let's go get groceries, Dad. Then you can show us where we're going to live. Okay?"

They walked past the liquor store, heading for The Shopping Basket, a large supermarket.

Her mother's voice rang inside Shannon's head.

Forgive him!

If only she could listen to her mother's plea.

Forgive him, Shannon.

Suddenly her mother was there in front of Shannon, beckoning to her with open arms. Marietta Riley had somehow sprung to life again. She looked young, healthy, strong.

"Mom, thank God. We're living in a new

town. It's called Port City. Dad got an apartment for us."

Mrs. Riley seemed to be floating atop a mist bank that rose from the ground. "Shannon, my death was so hard on him. He lost his mind for a while."

"Mom, I'm afraid. I've been afraid ever since you left. I don't want Dad to be the way he was before he went into the hospital. I couldn't take that again."

Her mother smiled, floating next to her daughter, embracing her with arms that felt like cool breezes from the ocean. "He was sick after my death, Shannon."

"But you're not dead, Mother. You're right here in front of me. You're alive."

"Shannon, forgive him. Believe in him. We all have weaknesses. You understand, don't you?"

Shannon nodded. "I suppose so, Mom. But—"

"Shannon, believe in him. Forgive him."

"Mom . . ."

A shiver ran through Shannon's body. Her mother's touch had suddenly grown cold. The young, healthy woman began to fade. She was replaced by the scrawny carcass that had withered away in the hospital bed.

Shannon felt a sense of panic. "Mom!"

"I must go, Shannon."

"No, please—stay—you aren't dead. You're alive. Don't leave me again."

The spectral face had transformed into a skeletal mask.

"Mom!"

"I must go, darling."

"No!"

Her mother's shape began to rise, filtering through the air like a ghostly vapor.

Shannon grabbed for her, but every trace of Mrs. Riley had vanished except for the faint echo of her voice.

Forgive him!

"Mom! No!"

Shannon sat up in her bed, shaking from the dream. She had seen her mother's face so clearly. It had been so real.

Forgive him.

"Yes, Mom," she said aloud. "I'll try."

Shannon suddenly realized that she had awakened in a bright room with white curtains and a white bedspread.

As her eyes focused, she felt a sudden sense of disassociation. Where was she? How had she come to be in this white room? This wasn't her aunt's house in Maine.

No, it was a townhouse apartment in Pitney Docks, part of the waterfront section of Port City.

They had arrived at the apartment after

shopping for groceries. When dinner was over, Shannon had fallen asleep almost immediately. She hadn't seen much of her new home, her new town, or the new school where she would start in less than two weeks.

Shannon threw off the covers and put one foot on the hardwood floor.

She felt rested, ready to begin exploring her new environment.

Shannon would find a lot of stuff, some of it none too pleasant.

FOUR

The Riley's second-floor, walk-up apartment was located in a newly renovated section of the waterfront. Shannon's room wasn't as large as her room in Manchester, but the white walls were clean and the hardwood floors had been recently stripped and polished. Shannon moved to the double windows that faced River Street. A puff of fresh sea air greeted her as she opened them.

Shannon stuck her head out, looking up and down River Street. To her left lay the shops and restaurants that had opened on the waterfront in May. The town of Port City was trying to make the pier area a showcase for tourists from Memorial Day to the end of foliage season. So far, the project had succeeded, at least partially.

When Shannon glanced to her right, she saw what remained of the old waterfront, a run-down, ramshackle line of abandoned warehouses and dilapidated storefronts. Shannon preferred to look back to her left, where the summer morning sparkled off the aquamarine surface of the Tide Gate River. Gulls circled lazily in the blue sky and minnows darted through the swirling currents of the river. In the middle of the village at Market Square, the bell in North Church rang seven times.

Shannon filled her lungs with salty air. It was a beautiful Sunday morning in a storybook place. She had to get out to explore. Hurrying to her suitcases, she began to unpack, filling the drawers of the small cherrywood chest. The place had come furnished with used but clean furniture that certainly didn't measure up to her mother's decorating.

Stop it, she told herself. Don't compare. *Forgive him.*

At least he's not drinking.

When she had emptied her suitcase, Shannon turned toward the black trunk. It contained her mother's keepsakes and memorabilia. Shannon gave a shudder, even in the warm breeze. She hadn't been able to bring herself to look in the trunk. Maybe her father would open it for her.

Forgive and forget.
"I can't forget, Mother."
She sighed.
"I just loved you too much."

Shannon began to dress in jeans and a T-shirt. She put on running shoes with thick cotton socks. After she brushed her long brown hair, Shannon stepped quietly into the living room of her new home.

Her father still snored in the back bedroom. Patrick had not yet risen from his tiny room. He had complained about the cramped enclosure at first, until Shannon had given him a dirty look. She didn't want her father to be bummed about anything. She wanted him to be happy, so he wouldn't go back to drinking again.

Creeping to the front door, Shannon let herself out and then tiptoed down the single flight of stairs. The foyer of the stairwell was well lighted and covered with a fresh coat of plaster. Shannon exited onto a narrow sidewalk that would take her to Market Square. She was tempted to go alone, to see her new town by herself for a solo impression.

Do I dare?

She glanced up at the second-story window. Should she leave a note for her father? No. She'd travel a couple of blocks and then return home.

As Shannon started along the waterfront, her stride became longer, more confident. Most of the shops were closed, but a small coffee shop enticed her in for a cup of hot chocolate and a muffin to go. Shannon paid for it with a ten-dollar bill that her father had given her for an allowance.

Maybe things will be better, she thought.

Back on the sidewalk, she sipped at the cocoa and strolled closer to the end of the block. River Street angled into Taylor Avenue, which would take her to Middle Road. Shannon hesitated, wondering if she should go on. Then her eyes found the sign that pointed the way to Fair Common Park. Shannon had seen the park from the car. It was such a nice place. And pretty close to her new school, Central Academy.

Gazing back toward her apartment, Shannon told herself that she wouldn't be gone long. Just a short jaunt to the park, sit on a bench, eat the muffin, and come home. She'd probably get back before Patrick and her father woke up. If she brought them muffins and coffee, they wouldn't even mind that she had been gone.

She started up Taylor Avenue, following a sidewalk that rose to the crest of Middle Road. She didn't have to walk far on Middle Road to reach the park. The green grass and full trees shimmered in the morning sun.

"This really is a great place," she told herself.

The park was deserted except for a few dog walkers. Shannon sat down on a green bench, nibbling at the muffin. When she finished, she stood up and gazed at the other side of the park.

A quick trip around the perimeter, then home. She began to shuffle along the grass, which still had shady areas that were covered with dew. Shannon tried not to be too hopeful, but her enthusiasm for Port City was growing every moment.

Maybe the worst is over, she hoped.

As she approached the opposite side of the park, Shannon became aware of a boy on a bicycle. He was riding slowly in her direction, coming from behind on the right side. Shannon stepped off the grass, onto the paved walkway. She tried to ignore the boy but he was already on her, pedaling and coasting so he could stay beside Shannon.

"Hi there," he said in a pleasant enough tone. "It's a really nice day, eh?"

Shannon ignored him. She didn't want to talk to a stranger, even if Port City was a friendly town. She managed to cast a sidelong glance in the boy's direction, sizing him up. He was tall and lanky, probably her age. His blue eyes seemed gentle and his long, sandy hair fell on his shoulders, making him appear to be harmless. But Shannon wasn't taking any chances.

"My name is Charley. What's your name?"

Shannon started walking away from him. "Leave me alone."

He followed her for a few feet. "Hey, I'm just trying to introduce myself."

"Well, don't!"

She quickened her pace, hoping that he would go away.

Charley put on the brakes. "Hey, I didn't know it was time for winter. Chill-ee!"

Shannon broke into a run, jogging in the direction of the street. The bicycle boy didn't come after her. He turned and rode off toward Market Square. Shannon figured he hadn't really been a threat, but she had to play it safe in a new town.

Any consternation Shannon felt about the encounter with the blond-haired bike rider vanished when she saw the green street sign pointing the way TO CENTRAL ACADEMY. She had only seen her new school from the car. Didn't she deserve a closer look? After all, she was the one who had to attend Central. Patrick, too.

Shannon glanced back toward town. She

was fairly certain that she could find her path back to the waterfront. Central Academy lay a few blocks away, ready for inspection.

I'll only take a few minutes and then head straight home, she thought. One quick look.

Shannon darted across the street, following Rockbury Lane, the same street her father had taken the day before.

Great! Her second day in town and she could already find her way around. Port City had definite possibilities.

When Shannon reached the edge of the school grounds, she stopped and put her hands on her hips.

She smiled at the red brick structures. "Excellent."

It was much better than Manchester High.

Crossing the street, she entered the campus, striding across a plush carpet of long grass. As she approached the classroom buildings, Shannon came into a large plaza, a gathering place with picnic tables and wooden benches. She hurried across the plaza, stealing a look into a classroom.

The rows of desks were neat and straight. Everything appeared to be brand new, including the chalkboard. Manchester High had been old and musty, patched with occasional graffiti. Maybe the Riley family had really gotten back on track.

You can't hold it against him forever, Shannon.

"I know, Mom."

Forgive and forget.

Shannon followed the line of the building until she reached the walkway that led to the gymnasium. Beyond the gym sat the rounded hump of the pool dome. Shannon had to wonder if juniors were allowed to go swimming. Were there open hours or phys ed classes like water polo and swimming competitions?

"This is going to be rad."

Suddenly, the bell in North Church began to toll. It rang nine times. Shannon had been gone for more than an hour. What if her father woke up and she wasn't there? She hadn't left a note and the phone hadn't been installed yet so there was no way for her to call him. She had to get home.

But which way was home?

She turned slowly, trying to figure out the proper direction. Exploring the school grounds had turned her around a little. She had come from Rockbury Lane, which appeared to be back to her right. She took one step before she saw the bicycle rolling out onto the campus plaza.

The blond kid had returned.

He came toward Shannon, pumping the pedals of the mountain bike.

She'd never be able to outrun him.

And even as she walked toward the street, the blond boy began to ride in a wide, concentric circle that gradually took him closer to her.

FIVE

Shannon froze in the middle of the plaza, watching as the bicycle drew closer. The boy had a narrow-eyed expression on his thin face. Shannon could see the yellow fuzz on his chin, as if he had tried to grow a goatee. A black T-shirt covered his torso, emblazoned with the silk screen of some heavy metal rock band that she did not recognize.

"You gonna tell me your name?" the boy asked.

Shannon shook her head. "I don't think so."

"Remember me? I'm Charley."

"Just leave me alone."

Charley suddenly stopped the bike and put his feet on the ground. He took a deep breath, leaning forward on the handle bars. He didn't look dangerous, though he now seemed a little hostile.

"I thought you were rude back there," he told her. "I mean, I just said hello. I only wanted to introduce myself."

"I—I'm sorry. I didn't mean to be rude." Her body trembled as she tried to be brave. "I'm just not used to talking to people I don't know."

Charley nodded, smiling. "Yeah, I understand. You're new here. Going to Central next year?"

Shannon glared at him. "That's none of your business."

"Just asking."

He began to pedal the bike again, running a circle around her.

"I'm leaving," Shannon demanded.

"Fine," the boy replied. "I won't stop you. I'm not one to be rude."

She started forward, ready to ignore him again.

"Hey," he called from the bicycle, "are you Shannon Riley?"

Shannon stopped dead in her tracks, wheeling to glare at him. "How did you—"

"I'm Charley," he told her, "Charley Cutshawl. My father is from Cutshawl Realty. He rented your father the apartment on River Street."

Shannon deflated a little, unable to hang

on to her anger now that she had a connection with the boy. "Oh. I see."

"Your father showed me a picture of you from his wallet. He's really proud of you."

Shannon blushed and lowered her eyes. "Thanks." She wondered if Charley knew anything about her father's problem.

Charley shrugged and turned the bike in her direction, coming by for a closer look. "Wow, you're a lot prettier than that picture. You're hot, Shannon."

"That's no concern of yours, Charley!"

He braked the bicycle, stopping directly in front of Shannon. "Hey, I just wanted to say hi before school starts."

Shannon's eyes narrowed. "Why?"

He sighed. "Because I'm nobody. I do a little surfing in the summer, when there are waves. And once school starts, the guys like Skip Bradley will be hitting on you pretty heavy. I won't be able to get close. I thought I'd introduce myself now. So you'll know who I am when school starts."

He sounded sincere enough.

Shannon nodded and offered a slight, scoffing laugh. "Okay, you've introduced yourself."

"Then I better go," Charley replied. "See ya."

He turned the bicycle away from her, pedaling toward the street.

Shannon suddenly realized that she had forgotten her way. "Wait, Charley!"

Braking abruptly, Charley spun back in her direction, riding to the rescue. "Yo, what?"

Shannon took a deep breath. "I'm lost. I have to get back to my apartment. My Dad doesn't know where I am."

"Cool. Follow me."

Charley rode slowly beside her, guiding Shannon back to Rockbury Lane. She insisted that she could find her way from there, but Charley kept tagging along, telling her all about Port City and Central Academy. It was a pretty cool town with concerts at the Civic Arena and a good beach. Central wasn't a bad school, but it sucked sometimes. The faculty were pretty strict, even though they never gave Charley a problem about his long hair. He liked English best, and sometimes wrote poems for extra credit. He had even published a poem in the *Central Academy Crier*, the school newspaper.

"Writing poetry makes everyone think I'm a wuss," he offered. "Do you think it's wimpy to write poetry? For a guy, I mean."

Shannon shook her head, becoming more impatient with him. "No, I don't think it's wimpy."

"Would you like to read my poems some-time?"

"Look, I have to get home, Charley. I mean, thanks for everything, but I have things to do."

"Hey, don't we all."

As they crossed Middle Road, Charley kept yakking in her ear, never letting up. He had a crush on her. She could see it in his eyes. Not that he was bad looking and he seemed sort of nice, if somewhat pesky. Shannon just wasn't ready to strike up a romance or a friendship this particular morning.

When they reached the other side of Middle Road, Shannon heard screeching tires as a Subaru wagon rounded the corner. Brakes squealed and the Subaru ground to a stop. Mr. Riley jumped out, shouting to his daughter.

"Shannon, where did you go? I woke up and you weren't there."

Shannon blushed red and grimaced. "I'm sorry, Dad, I—I went for a walk and then I met Charley here."

Charley nodded to her father. "Hello, Mr. Riley. Remember me? I was with my dad when he rented you the apartment."

Mr. Riley's dire expression slacked into an embarrassed smile. "Uh, yes, of course. Shannon—"

She stepped toward him. "'Dad, I'm sorry. I woke up early so I went for a walk. I was on the way back—"

"Hey, it was my fault, Mr. Riley," Charley offered. "We got to talking and—"

Shannon glared at him. "I don't need you to testify on my behalf, Charley."

Mr. Riley patted her on the shoulder. "Hey, it's okay. You made a new friend. Charley, would you like to join us for breakfast? My treat?"

Shannon bit her lip. She didn't want Charley to come along. True, he was sort of cute, but he had been a nuisance so far.

Charley seemed to sense her reluctance. "Uh, no, that's okay, Mr. Riley. I've already eaten breakfast."

"How about dinner?" her father persisted. "I make a pretty mean dish of spaghetti and meatballs."

Charley shook his head, turning the bike up Middle Road. "Maybe some other time, sir. See ya around, Shannon. Don't forget me when we meet in the hallway."

"Sure, Charley, I—"

Before she could exact a proper reply, he was gone, pedaling his way toward Market Square.

"Nice kid," Mr. Riley offered. "And as for you, young lady—"

She glanced at her father, wondering if

he was going to fly off the handle, the way he had lost it before his treatment. "Dad, I'm sorry I—"

He waved her off, smiling. "It's all right, honey. Just next time, leave a note. I couldn't stand to lose you. I . . ." His voice trailed off.

"Oh, Dad—"

Suddenly, Patrick's voice filled the morning air. "Shannon's got a boyfriend!"

He was hanging half in and half out of the Subaru's passenger side window.

Shannon waved her fist at him. "Shut up, you little dweeb."

Mr. Riley shook his head. "It's so good to hear you kids arguing. I think we're gonna be so happy here."

I hope so, Shannon thought. I really hope so.

"Let's go to Howard Johnson's and get some breakfast," Mr. Riley offered.

Shannon smiled. "Sure, Dad."

They piled into the Subaru and started up Rockbury Lane.

When Shannon saw the school again, she leaned back and sighed.

"What's wrong?" her father asked.

"Nothing," Shannon replied.

In fact, there really was nothing wrong.

For the first time since her mother's death, Shannon actually felt happy.

She was looking forward to attending Central Academy.

Where her entire life would be turned upside down and inside out.

SIX

Shannon's first day at school got off to a rollicking start. As she strolled onto the school grounds dressed in a pair of jeans and a white blouse, she heard several catcalls from the boys who lingered in the junior parking lot. The comments were rude and immature, but somehow energetic and encouraging.

"Hey, gorgeous!"

"Whoa, major fox on the loose."

"New blood at Central."

Patrick sneered at the boys. "They can't talk to you like that, Shannon."

"Hush, they don't mean anything by it. Come on, we have to find someone in charge."

Mr. Riley had not accompanied them to Central. He had to be at work before eight,

44

so he couldn't help them enroll. Their father claimed that he had written to their old school district, requesting that the records be forwarded to Central Academy. Shannon still wasn't sure that he could be entirely trusted.

At the administration office, the secretary informed Shannon and Patrick that their records had indeed arrived from Manchester, and that they could see a guidance counselor immediately to arrange their schedules. By the time all of the particulars had been completed, it was time for homeroom. Shannon stood up at the first bell and said good-bye to Patrick, assuring him that he need not be as scared as he looked.

The morning flew by with no real problems.

First period English yielded Mr. Hanks, a recent college graduate with a penchant for poetry. Of course, Charley Cutshawl, who sat across the aisle from her, liked Mr. Hanks immediately. Charley also sent a few moon-eyed stares in Shannon's direction. She ignored him, hoping that he would give up eventually. Not that she didn't want to be friends with Charley. Shannon just wasn't in the market for a *boyfriend*.

Second and third period were serious.

Her counsellor had talked her into taking advanced biology and algebra. Shannon wasn't sure she could handle either class, but she liked both teachers and she was willing to try.

She got a bit of a break during fourth period, which was her film appreciation class. Easing into a desk, Shannon took a deep breath and exhaled. This was her only elective class and it led up to her lunch hour. After lunch, she had to tackle geography and beginning Latin. Central Academy stressed academics, her counsellor had told her. If she did the work and earned the grades, Shannon could easily go on to an Ivy League college.

"Let me just get through my junior year," she muttered to herself. "I'd settle for that."

"Tough day, Princess?"

The voice was deep, resonant.

Shannon looked up quickly, gazing into a pair of devastating brown eyes. A boy smiled at her, revealing perfect white teeth that had been shaped by braces and capping. His black hair was combed back in thick waves and he was dressed in tan chinos and a white shirt with an alligator. A real prep. And probably the most handsome boy that Shannon had ever seen in her life.

He sat across the aisle from her, keeping up that pearly smile. "I'm Skip. Skip Bradley. Welcome to Central."

Shannon nodded shyly. "Thanks."

"Are you Shannon? The new girl?"

Her eyes widened. "How did—"

He waved at her. "Hey, I heard about you before you even started here."

She smiled. "You did?"

"Sure. Any time a girl who looks like you . . . oh, hey, I'm sorry, I didn't mean anything. You know, some guys can be so crude. Like that dweeb, you know, the poetry wuss, Charley. He's a friend of yours, isn't he?"

"Uh, yes," Shannon replied quickly. "But just a friend."

"Hey, I didn't mean to call him a dweeb—"

"That's all right," Shannon replied. "Sometimes I call him that myself."

Skip laughed. "You're funny."

And you're a total scorcho mega-hunk!

"Uh, thanks," she replied, her tongue tied in knots. "I—"

The teacher walked in as the bell rang, calling the class to order.

Skip Bradley flashed one last friendly grin in her direction, then turned to face the teacher.

He seemed like a real gentleman.

Shannon wanted to know more about the wavy-haired boy with the kind, brown eyes.

The Central cafeteria buzzed with juniors comparing notes on the first day of school. Shannon came out of the line with her tray and started to search the lunchroom for a familiar face. But she didn't find him—he found her.

"Shannon, hey, there you are. Haven't seen you since first period English."

Charley stepped up next to her, following Shannon toward a row of tables. She was actually glad to see him. Maybe Charley could answer a few questions for her.

"Wanna sit together?" Charley asked.

"Sure," she replied. "There's a spot."

As soon as she sat down, Shannon noticed that Skip was sitting across the room from her. He had landed at a table with some other boys. And he was looking at Shannon, nodding and smiling.

Shannon blushed, smiled, and then avoided his gaze.

"How's your first day so far?" Charley asked.

Shannon picked up her fork. "Fine." She poked at her salad, though she wasn't interested in eating lunch anymore. Skip had captured her imagination.

What was he really like?

Did he have a girlfriend?

She lifted her green eyes, smiling bashfully. "I've met a lot of people today."

"Cool. Anybody I know?"

"Well, Skip Bradley."

Charley froze, dropping his hamburger. "That didn't take long, did it?"

Shannon leaned back in her chair. "What?"

"Skip always checks out new girls. He's a real hound, Shannon. He doesn't have a sincere bone in his body. He uses people like the rest of those prep types from Prescott Estates."

Her brow wrinkled. "Prescott Estates?"

"Yeah, it's this fancy neighborhood over on the other side of town," Charley replied with disgust. "Stay away from Skip and his goons."

Shannon peered over Charley's shoulder for a moment, studying Skip. He seemed so gentle and sincere. Charley was just jealous that Shannon had paid attention to someone else.

"He seems nice enough," Shannon offered. "Could you just be a little envious, Charley?"

Charley pointed his finger at her. "Look, I care about you, Shannon. I mean it."

She shrugged it off, looking down at her

tray. "Well, if you don't want to tell me—"

Charley slammed his hand on the table, startling her. "I'll tell you. Here goes. Look over my shoulder. See those kids sitting with Skip?"

Shannon peered at Skip's table again. "Yeah?"

"Start with the little one," Charley said. "The one with greasy red hair. His name is Rollie Danova. He'll steal anything he can get his hands on. He's been away to the juvenile detention center twice."

"Are you making this up?" Shannon challenged. "I mean, he's so cute."

"They're all cute," Charley continued. "The big guy, the one who looks like he's on steroids. Andy Rothman. He's a gun freak. Almost got thrown out of school last year for bringing a pistol to career day."

He couldn't be telling her the truth!

But he didn't let up. "The kid with the flat nose—" Shannon's eyes fell on a lean kid with blond hair. "—that's Peter McEvoy. Likes to fight. Get a look at his hands sometime. He's got knuckles on his knuckles."

"But he's dressed like a preppie," Shannon offered. "They all dress like preppies."

"Don't let that fool you, Shannon. They don't play. And Skip's the ringleader."

"You left one out," Shannon said. "Who's the chubby kid with curly black hair?"

Charley scoffed. "Guy Baines. He's a glue freak. Got caught snorting paint remover in wood shop. A real crisp dude. He's been fried every way possible."

Shannon leaned forward, dropping her fork on her tray. "You have such a low opinion of everyone but yourself, Charley."

He gaped at her. "What'd I do?"

"You fed me a bunch of garbage," she told him in a hostile voice. "You're jealous of Skip so you slam him and his friends, telling me all those lies."

"Hey, you wanted the truth . . . where are you going?"

Shannon stood up quickly, grabbing her tray. "I'm going to join Skip and his friends."

Charley grabbed at her. "No, you can't. They're bad news."

Shannon drew back. "They can't be half as bad as you say. How could they stay in a good school like Central if they were such holy terrors?"

"Don't do it, Shannon, please—"

Shannon started toward Skip's table. "Good-bye, Charley. It was nice knowing you."

"You're making a big mistake, Shannon!"

But Shannon only smiled at Skip and headed in his direction.

She had no way of knowing that Charley was right.

Sorry we could not buy
your item.
OrderNumber:3287544
Reason: Rou
Date: 2024-09-10

0007455123 4

0007455 1234 9

SEVEN

Shannon didn't feel at all nervous about approaching the table full of boys. She knew that Charley had to be wrong. Charley just wanted to be part of the in-crowd, but they wouldn't have him. Shannon wasn't thinking of popularity, however. She just wanted to look into Skip Bradley's soulful brown eyes.

Skip stood up as she drew closer. "Hi, Shannon. How did you like the film we saw in class?"

She shrugged. "It was all right."

Skip gestured to the others. "These are some friends of mine. Rollie, Guy, Andy, and Peter."

Shannon flashed her best smile and nodded at them. "I don't mean to barge in—"

Skip laughed. "No way. Sit down."

"Oh, I don't want to intrude," Shannon replied. "I just wanted to thank you for being so nice to me in film class. It's tough being new."

"I understand, Shannon," Skip told her. "We've all been there. I changed middle schools three times."

Rollie Danova snorted derisively. "Yeah, he kept gettin' thrown out!"

Skip shot a frosty glance in Rollie's direction. "Hey, you boys were just leaving, weren't you?"

Rollie returned the hostile glare. "We were here first."

Guy Baines stood up, grabbing Rollie's shoulder. "Come on, lightning boy, you need some fresh air."

Rollie stood up, drawing away from the chubby boy. "I'm on the way. Don't wrinkle the clothes."

Rollie brushed past Guy, who followed him outside to the open plaza in the middle of the campus.

Peter McEvoy jumped on his feet, waving politely at Shannon. "Excuse my friends," he said with a smile. "I don't think they've had their raw meat today."

Andy Rothman was right next to Peter, studying Shannon with beady eyes. "Yo, we're out of here. So long, stone fox. I'll see you later."

They departed for the plaza as well.

Skip offered Shannon the chair again. "Do you like my friends? I made them myself." His laughter was irresistible.

Shannon eased into her chair, casting a quick glance at Charley, who watched them from the other side of the cafeteria.

I'll show him, she thought.

"I really like Central so far," Shannon offered.

Skip leaned back in his chair. "You know, you could be a cheerleader. I could get you a tryout."

Shannon shook her head. "I've never been interested in that sort of thing. But I do like football. Are you on the team?"

Skip seemed to scoff at the idea. "Nah. I don't want to end up with my nose on the wrong side of my face. And my dad would kill me if I got this dental work knocked out. I'd hate to ruin my appearance."

Shannon could barely hear him, she was so absorbed in his good looks. Her heart had begun to pound. What sort of secrets lay behind those brown eyes? He seemed deep, complex, intriguing.

"Shannon, there's something I wanted to ask you—"

But the bell rang, calling them to class. Shannon bit her lip. Skip had been on the verge of asking her to go out on a date. She just knew it.

He smiled bashfully and stood up. "Better get to class. Can I call you?"

Shannon suddenly felt paralyzed. "I—I don't have a phone yet. Sorry . . ."

"Then I'll see you around."

He offered a wink before he strode off toward the main hallway.

Shannon slammed her hand on the table. "Damn!" He had been so close to asking.

She took a deep breath. It didn't matter. She'd see him again. And he'd ask the next time.

Shannon glanced in the direction of the table where Charley was sitting. He grimaced and shook his head. Shannon smirked at him. With a scowl, Charley rose from the table and stormed into the corridor.

Spoilsport, Shannon thought.

She liked Skip, not Charley.

She could like whomever she wanted to like.

The rest of the day flew by like a pleasant dream. Her geography teacher was a nice woman in her late fifties, a matronly dynamo named Hattie Jones. Latin I seemed fairly easy, since Shannon had already taken three years of Spanish in middle school. The Latin instructor was a nice, skinny man with thick glasses—Mr. St. Cloud. His voice was somewhat irritating with its high pitch, but Shannon found him to be even-tempered and professional.

When the final bell rang, Shannon walked out of the classroom with a satisfied grin on her lovely face. The first day of school had been excellent. Everything had fallen into place.

Except Charley Cutshawl.

"Hey, Shannon, over here!"

She flinched, wincing at the imposing tone of Charley's voice. He had been leaning against a wall of lockers on the other side of the hall. Shannon tried to walk fast but the corridor was crowded, so Charley caught up easily.

"I saw you at lunch with Skip," he offered.

Shannon glanced sideways at him, scowling back. "I saw you looking at me."

"Shannon, listen to me—"

She turned a corner, trying to leave him in her wake.

"Shannon!"

Charley ran through the hall to catch her. He bumped into one small kid and almost knocked him down. Charley didn't even stop to help. He was too intent on reaching Shannon.

She stopped at her new locker, spinning the combination lock.

Charley leaned on the locker next to hers. "Shannon, okay, listen to me—"

"Charley, leave me alone."

He grabbed her wrist. "Listen to me! Charley—"

"Please!"

She jerked her hand away. "Drop dead." After she had stored some books and taken others, she slammed the locker door and started for the exit at the end of the hallway.

"Shannon—"

"Go away, Charley."

"Shannon, okay, I admit it. I have a crush on you. I mean, you're totally stoked, a real babe. And you're nice too."

The compliments would have meant more coming from Skip.

Instead, they were coming from Charley. "You're great, Shannon, but you've got to listen. This doesn't have anything to do with me liking you. Skip is bad news. Ask around about him."

Shannon cleared the exit door, moving into the junior parking area with Charley still dogging her steps. She began to look for Patrick in the crowd. They were supposed to walk home together.

"Shannon, you've got to—"

Shannon spun to face him. "Charley, leave me alone."

"Shannon, I'm not jealous—"

She glared into his blue eyes. "You're not?"

He looked away. "Okay, I'm jealous. But this is different. Skip has a bad reputation with girlfriends. One of his steadies ended up in a mental hospital. I swear!"

Shannon shook her head, holding up her palm. "Charley, just get away from me now or I'll report you to the police."

"Police?"

"I mean, you're coming on like some mad stalker here. You won't leave me alone."

A hurt expression spread over his face. "Shannon . . ."

"Look, at first I thought we could be friends, Charley, but you're out of control. I can't deal with it."

His face suddenly turned a bright shade of crimson. "Fine, if that's the way you want it. Just don't come to me when everything blows up in your—"

"Hey guys, what's happening?"

Patrick strolled up, grinning dumbly at them, neglecting to perceive the tension between his sister and the long-haired boy.

"Great school, huh?" Patrick offered in a friendly tone.

Charley scowled at him. "Yeah, just great." He stomped off to the bicycle parking area.

"What's his problem?" Patrick asked.

Shannon shook her head, trying to forget Charley. "Nothing. So, how'd you like it?"

Patrick was all smiles. "I love it, Sis. This is a great school. They have a science club and everything."

Shannon's good mood returned with such force that she could barely contain her enthusiasm. "It's rad. Come on, let's go home. Dad gets out of work in a couple of hours. I can't wait to tell him."

They started for the sidewalk, moving only a few steps before the car horn sounded. Shannon looked back to see a bright red Mazda Miata convertible rolling along the edge of the junior parking lot. The convertible top was down and Skip Bradley sat behind the wheel.

Skip nodded. "Hi, there. Need a ride?" He leaned on the top of the car door, brandishing his liquid smile.

Patrick frowned. "Who's that?"

My new boyfriend if all goes well, Shannon thought.

"Just a friend," she replied.

Skip looked at Patrick. "What have we here?"

"My little brother," Shannon replied. "Wow, that's a nice car."

He waved at her. "Come on, I'll give you a ride home."

She nodded at her brother. "What about Patrick?"

"Yeah, what about *me?*"

Skip grimaced. "I don't think there's room enough for three of us. This *is* a sports car after all."

Shannon felt a burst of anger. First the bell had ruined her shot at Skip, now Patrick was getting in the way. She had to be alone with him. He was going to ask her out. She knew it!

A car horn sounded behind Skip. Another vehicle, a huge tank of a station wagon, edged up to the bumper of the Miata, nudging it gently. Rollie Danova had his hands on the wheel. The other three guys were with him.

Rollie hung his head out the window. "Hey, Bradley, get that crate moving."

Skip looked back at them. "How about giving the kid a ride home so I can show Shannon my car?"

Rollie grimaced and rolled his eyes. "Come on—"

Patrick glanced at his sister. "I don't

want to ride with them," he said in a low voice.

Shannon gave him a pleading look with her green eyes. "Just this once, Patrick. Please!"

"Help me out here," Skip said good-naturedly. "I've just met the woman of my dreams, Danova."

Shannon blushed, smiling broadly. She liked the sound of that: *woman of my dreams.* And he looked so good behind the wheel of the Miata.

Rollie smirked. "Come on, squirt."

"I think he means you, Patrick," Skip said.

Patrick shook his head. "Uh, I don't think—"

Skip nodded toward the station wagon. "Go on."

Patrick sighed. "Shannon . . . ?"

She urged him toward Skip's buddies. "Go on, it'll be fine. Won't it be fine, Skip?"

"Sure. My buds are cool. And I'll bring your sister straight home, Patrick. I just want to talk to her."

Patrick walked reluctantly toward the station wagon. The rear door flew open. When Patrick was near the door, a strong hand reached out and snatched him into the car. The tires squealed and the wagon sped around the Miata, making for the street as the back door swung shut.

Shannon was taken aback by Rollie's reckless driving. "Are you sure my brother will be all right?"

"You have my personal guarantee, Princess. Get in."

Shannon hesitated. "Uh, Skip—"

He smiled. "Oh, I see."

He climbed out of the car and walked to the passenger side, opening the door for Shannon. "Your carriage awaits."

She laughed at him. "Wow, are you for real?"

"Go out with me Friday night and find out."

Shannon suddenly felt light-headed. He had asked her, just like that. No, he had commanded her. And all she had to do was say yes.

"I'll think about it on the ride home," Shannon replied.

Skip's jaw dropped for a moment. Shannon walked around to the other side of the Miata, climbing into the passenger seat. Skip closed the door and jumped behind the wheel. He tore off through the parking lot, exiting onto Rockbury Lane.

Shannon loved the sensation of the wind in her dark hair. She leaned back in the seat, watching Port City as it flew by. For the first time since her mother's death, she felt free of remorse, devoid of pain. Every cell in her body vibrated with a chord struck in complete harmony.

"There's this dance on Friday night," Skip started. "After the football game. Would you like to go?"

Shannon mustered her courage playing a bit coy. "Oh? What about the game? Do you have another date for that?"

Did I really say that!? she thought. *What if I blow it?*

Skip looked straight ahead, his face sort of perplexed. "Well, I was going to go to the game with the guys . . ."

Shannon shrugged. "Fine. What time do you want to pick me up for the dance?" She'd take her brother to the game. Or a new friend if she made any others this lucky week.

"I'll come by your house around seven-thirty," he replied. "Show me where you live."

She guided him through the streets of Port City, terminating the delightful jaunt at the waterfront.

Skip pulled the Miata in front of the apartment building, turning off the motor. "Can I come up?"

Shannon hesitated at the casual nature of his request. "Uh, no, I—"

A car horn sounded behind them.

Shannon looked back to see the station wagon pulling next to the curb. Her brother seemed to eject himself from the backseat. He landed on the sidewalk, almost landing on his face, but he managed to regain his balance before he hit the ground. The station wagon roared off with Rollie and the rest of Skip's wild friends. Patrick staggered toward the front door, glaring at Shannon before he went in.

Shannon stared at Skip as he sat behind the steering wheel. "What did they do to him?"

"Nothing, they were just horsing around, Shannon. They're regular guys. It'll do your brother good to hang out with them. Might bring him out of his shell."

His voice sounded so wise. "You might be right. Thanks for the ride, Skip."

She started to get out of the car.

His hand fell on her shoulder. "Hey, are we on for the dance?"

She nodded. "Of course, seven-thirty."

He jerked his hand away. "Sorry. I—I didn't mean to touch you like that. I—"

"It's all right," she replied.

Shannon leaned back into the car and gave him a peck on the cheek. "See you in school tomorrow."

"Sure."

She got out, running to the stairs, not looking back. She was afraid he might disappear forever if she looked back. Shannon didn't want the dream to be over. She wanted this great feeling to last.

When she entered the living room, Patrick sat slumped on the couch. "What a bunch of jerks," he said. "Real knuckledraggers. Nice call, Sis."

Her eyes narrowed. "Did they hurt you?"

He scoffed. "No. But they're stupid. One of them was smoking a cigarette. Are you going out with that guy in the fancy car? Mr. Wonderful?"

Shannon smiled mischievously. "Not that it's any of your business—but I am."

"You have to ask Dad," Patrick warned. "If Mr. Wonderful—"

"His name is Skip," she replied defensively. "Skip Bradley. He lives in the best neighborhood in Port City."

"If he's anything like his friends—"

"Well he's not, Patrick! And don't say anything to Dad. I'll ask him myself."

Patrick sighed. "I'm going to do my homework. I wish we had a TV." He shuffled into his room and closed the door.

Shannon hurried into her own bedroom. She quickly opened the windows, letting in the sea air. Gazing down on River Street on a bright September afternoon, she realized

she had never expected to feel this happy
ever again.

"Skip Bradley," she whispered to the
breeze.

Skip had to be a nickname. He probably
had some weird first name that she could
make fun of between kisses. What could it
be? Something strange and exotic that only
she would know.

Shannon's elation faded when she saw
the movement of the bicycle as it inched
slowly along the other side of the street.

Charley!

He was watching her.

She turned away from the window, moving toward her bed. A few seconds elapsed
before she noticed the pink envelope that
had been dropped on her pillow. Someone
had been in her room. Maybe it was a note
from her father. There was no name on the
envelope though. Shannon picked it up
and tore out the white three-by-five card.

The message was simple: "Stay away
from Skip or you'll regret it." No signature.

She wadded the note into a little ball of
paper. *Charley!*

How had he gotten into her room? She
shuddered. He had actually touched her
pillow. How creepy!

Shannon ran back to the window and
gazed out on River Street. She looked for

the bicycle, but it was no longer there. Charley had disappeared into the afternoon shadows.

Tossing the wadded note into the street, Shannon closed the windows and then ran into the living room to lock the front door.

I'll tell my father, she thought.

She hesitated. No. Telling Mr. Riley about the incident would only upset him. Shannon wanted to share all the *good* news about her first day at Central. She didn't want to put any more pressure on him.

Besides, Charley probably wasn't dangerous. Maybe she should tell Skip about him. Skip looked like he could handle himself pretty well.

She flopped on her bed, staring at the ceiling, picturing Skip's face.

He was so handsome and gentle.

Nothing would stop her from dating Skip Bradley.

Nothing.

Not even restless nightmares about her dead mother.

EIGHT

The vapors rose around Marietta Riley, lifting her into the air. Shannon also floated off the bizarre terrain of the dreamscape, spinning in slow motion, following her mother's spirit toward the dark firmament. It seemed so easy and natural that they should be together in this ethereal place.

"Mom, I have a new boyfriend."

"I know," Mrs. Riley's voice declared. "But I don't approve of him. He's not for you, Shannon."

Shannon was dumbfounded. "Mom, he's great. He's handsome, polite, he drives a nice car."

"What's inside this boy?" Mrs. Riley asked.

"Mom, I told you—he's great looking,

he's sweet, and he drives a new car. He's wonderful."

Mrs. Riley smiled, patient with her daughter. "Shannon, those are all surface qualities. What's he made of inside? What about his character?"

Shannon became angry in her dream, the way she had become angry in real life, when her mother questioned her boy-friends. "You don't understand me!"

"Shannon, please—"

"I hate you!"

"Shannon, listen to me—"

But her mother's form had already begun to fade, changing into the specter that had been lying on the deathbed in the hospital. She was leaving Shannon again. Suddenly, Shannon felt a deep sense of remorse.

"Mom, no!"

Mrs. Riley shook the skeletal mask that had been her face a few seconds earlier. "It's too late, Shannon."

"Mom . . ."

"You showed your disrespect for me once too often. That's why I died. It was your fault."

"Mom, I didn't mean to—"

"Good-bye, Shannon. Remember it was all your fault . . ."

"Please, Mom—"

". . . All your fault . . ."

"No, you were sick—"

". . . Your fault . . .!"

Her mother disappeared.

Shannon heard laughter. She turned to see a choir of people, mocking her with hellish music. They were all there, the new and old characters of her life. Her father and brother, Skip and his friends, all her new teachers.

She couldn't understand what they were saying, but Shannon knew that she had done wrong. She had caused her mother's death. It was all her fault.

"No!"

Shannon dug her way out of the nightmare, waking to a bright morning. Sweat pearled on her face and she felt ragged, as if she hadn't even slept. Her eyes flickered toward the clock on her nightstand. She had slept through the alarm. She was going to be late for her second day at Central Academy.

"Shannon," her brother called. "I'm ready to leave!"

She leapt out of bed, certain that it would be a tough day. Her mood was horrible. She kept hearing her mother's voice in her head, telling her not to trust Skip.

It really wasn't a great way to start the day.

• • •

"Shannon, sit with us!"

Erin Clifford, captain of the Central cheerleaders, waved to Shannon from the "cool" table where all the cheerleaders sat. Everybody knew Shannon after a mere two days of classes. They also knew that she was going out with Skip, that he was taking her to the big dance after the football game. Her popularity had soared in less than forty-eight hours.

Shannon enjoyed all of the attention, particularly the friendliness of Erin and her crowd. Somehow, she fit in already, as if she had attended Central for years. Of course, she didn't know all the names and faces yet, but that would come in time.

"Here," Erin called, "you can sit next to me."

Shannon strode toward the perky blonde who pulled out her chair. When Shannon sat down, the other girls said hello and began to make small talk. They wanted to know where Shannon had come from, how she liked Central, how she felt about going out with Skip Bradley.

Shannon replied in a pleasant voice, happy to be among friends so quickly. She told the truth about her own life for the most part, omitting her father's alcoholism and rehabs. She played it cool about Skip, only hinting that she had a major crush on him.

"Watch that snake," Erin said playfully.

Shannon's eyes narrowed a little. "What do you mean?"

"Skip has been out with *everyone!*"

"Yeah," another girl rejoined, "nobody has been able to tame him yet. He's a wild one, Shannon."

Shannon figured they were simply pulling her leg. "I could be the one," she offered.

A round of laughter met her remark.

"It could happen!" she insisted good-naturedly.

They continued talking about the football game and the dance. Shannon was having a great time, at least until she spotted the pair of intense blue eyes that stared back at her from another table. Charley Cutshawl watched her as she ate lunch with her new friends.

Dork, Shannon thought.

She grimaced, gave a defeated sigh and dropped her fork onto the salad plate.

Erin glanced sideways at her. "What's wrong?"

"Nothing," Shannon replied. "Just this creepy kid. Charley Cutshawl. He has a crush on me."

Erin shrugged. "He's a dink. Forget

about him. Or tell Skip. Skip'll take him out."

Shannon shook her head. "No, you're right. He's a dink. I just hope he isn't dangerous."

"No way," Erin assured her. "He's a wimp. A dweeb. A geek. Check him off your list."

Shannon pretended to ignore Charley, though a passing glance every minute or so caught his blue-eyed stare.

When the bell rang, Shannon rose quickly and headed for her geography class. Latin was next. She became lost in a vocabulary exercise, forgetting about Charley until she reached her locker at the end of the day.

This time, the note wasn't in an envelope. It had been taped together, triple folded and her name had been written on the front of the blue paper in a fancy script. The handwriting was different from the first note.

Shannon tore open the paper, only to find three words scrawled in the same elegant hand. *Don't do it.*

"Damn you, Charley."

He had someone working with him. A girl. Shannon gave a shudder, remembering what Charley had said about Skip.

One of Skip's girlfriends had ended up in a mental institution.

No, that had to be a lie.

Charley was the one who belonged in a mental institution.

He should be committed!

Shannon wadded up the note and found the nearest trash can.

She went outside to meet Patrick and they started home. She kept looking for Skip, but he didn't show. In fact, she hadn't seen him since fourth period class, where he had been kind and attentive.

As they crossed Middle Road, a bicycle whipped past them, coming so close that Shannon felt a rush of air.

Patrick's eyes widened. "Hey, that was Charley."

"Shut up, Patrick!"

Charley disappeared into the shadows on the other side of Middle Road.

Shannon bit her lip, angry at herself for letting Charley instill doubts in her mind. If one of Skip's old girlfriends had been committed to the cracker factory, it would be easy for Shannon to check out the truth. A few phone calls, asking around. She could even ask Erin.

No, that would be going behind Skip's back, she thought. But she had to know the truth.

She knew what she had to do.

Shannon had already decided to face Skip, to ask him personally about the ugly rumor that Charley had planted in her brain.

NINE

Friday night did not come soon enough for Shannon. The week had dragged on with the promise of her date with Skip hanging over her head. But the fateful hour had finally arrived, urging Shannon to the mirror for a discerning look at her reflection. She took inventory, wishing that she had been able to spend more than five dollars on makeup. Her father still hadn't drawn his first paycheck, so things were tight for the Riley family.

Shannon picked up the eyeliner pencil, touching the lip to her tongue before she used it to line the lower half of her right eye. Shannon sighed, stepping back, and shook her head. The black line was too much. A dab of cold cream and a tissue erased the dark line. She grabbed the hairbrush again, stroking her thick tresses.

I'll just have to go without a lot of makeup, she told herself.

A shiver spread through her lean body. She studied the soft shadows of her face. Everything had happened so unexpectedly. It was almost as if she had reclaimed her old life, before her mother had passed away.

Did she dare to hope that she could actually regain some sense of normalcy in her life?

"I'm so lucky," she said to the mirror.

One week at school and she already had a date with the best-looking boy in her class. She loved Port City and Central Academy. She cared about her brother and her father too. If only she could sustain the good feelings and the sense of well-being that had lifted her from the darkness.

The phone rang, startling Shannon for a moment. It had only been installed that day, so she hadn't gotten used to the ringing yet. In the living room, her brother answered the phone and then called to her.

"Hey, Sis, it's for you."

Shannon's brow wrinkled. For her? No one had the new phone number, not even Skip. She hurried into the living room to pick up the receiver.

"Hello?"

"Shannon, this is Charley."

She grimaced, casting a glance at Patrick who had waited to snoop on her call. "Charley, what do you want? And how did you get this number?"

"Ever hear of directory assistance? Shannon, please, you've got to listen to me. Don't go to the dance tonight with Skip. He's not the kind of guy you think he is—"

"Oh, and I suppose you are?" Shannon challenged.

"Her name was Katie," Charley went on. "Skip went out with her for almost a year. At the end, they took her babbling to the loony bin. You don't want to end up like her."

"Leave me alone, Charley!"

"Shannon, you've got to listen. They never pinned anything on Skip, but everyone knows that he's the reason Katie went crazy. If you don't believe me—"

"Drop dead, Charley!"

She slammed down the phone. How dare he call her right before her big date? Some nerve. If he didn't stop bothering her, Shannon would report him to the authorities.

"What's wrong?" Patrick asked.

"Nothing. Where's Dad?"

"He walked down to the store," Patrick replied.

"I thought you two were going to the football game," Shannon said. "Did you change your mind?"

Patrick shrugged. "No. Dad didn't want to go. I listened on the radio. Central won, twenty-one to nothing."

Shannon smiled. Skip would probably be in a good mood if the home team won. She was ready to dance the night away, at least until the phone rang again.

Shannon jumped and glared at Patrick. "Answer it!"

Patrick reluctantly picked up. "Hello? Charley—"

Shannon shook her head. "Tell him I'm in the shower," she whispered. "Then hang up."

Patrick hesitated. "Uh, she can't come to the phone. Can I take a message?"

Shannon bit her lip. Charley was really starting to become a nuisance. She remembered the note from her locker. And everywhere she went at school, Charley seemed to be there, gawking at her with those creepy blue eyes.

Patrick covered the mouthpiece with his hand. "Charley says to tell you not to go out with Skip. He's—"

A burst of anger made her reach for the

phone. "You listen to me, Charley. You're the one with the problem! If you don't leave me alone, I'm going to tell the police." She hung up before Charley could say another word.

"Turn off the ringer!" she blared at her brother. "And don't turn it back on until tomorrow!"

Patrick threw out his hands. "Why are you yelling at *me?*"

"Charlie is a creep!"

Patrick offered a derisive snort. "Yeah? Well, he seems a lot nicer than those goons who hang out with your new boyfriend."

"What do you know?" she snapped back at him. "You're just a pimply-faced geek anyway!"

She stormed back into her room, slamming the door behind her. Charley made her furious with his accusations against Skip. Charley was just jealous. Yet, his cautionary words rang in her head, the only downside of her new life in Port City.

Katie . . . loony bin.

You don't want to end up like her.

Shannon caught another glimpse of her image in the mirror. She looked great in the white sweater and tan slacks. She was ready for the most important night of her life. If only Charley hadn't tainted her joy with the doubts that nagged her.

"I have to ask Skip," she said to the mirror. "He'll tell me the truth."

As she turned away from the looking glass, the bell in North Church began to toll the hour. It was already eight o'clock. Skip had told her he would arrive at seven-thirty. He was late. Or had he stood her up?

Rushing to the window, Shannon opened the casement and peered out at the street. A cool, September breeze blew over the waterfront, giving her a chill. The street was empty. Skip's car had not arrived at the curb in front of her place. She had given him explicit directions to the apartment. Why hadn't he shown?

Shannon pulled back, slamming the window shut, never noticing the blond boy who rode his bicycle along the waterfront. If she had seen Charley, she probably would've thrown something at him. But she could only pace in her room now, wondering if the date would ever happen.

The minutes passed slowly, torturously. Skip did not arrive. The bell in Market Square sounded the half hour. He wasn't coming. She wasn't good enough for him. He was blowing her off.

Shannon opened the window again, staring out at the street. Someone meandered up the sidewalk. It was her father and he

was drinking from a bottle of dark liquid.
Shannon managed to duck back inside
before he saw her.

He was drinking again.

It was just like the party, when he hu-
miliated her in front of her friends, when
he had ruined her life.

To make it worse, a car stopped outside,
killing the engine in front of the entrance
to the apartment building.

Shannon had to look. She peeked
through a corner of the windowpane. Her
heart fluttered.

Skip opened the car door and stepped
out onto the sidewalk. Mr. Riley approached him, smiling and speaking in a
low voice that Shannon could not decipher.
What if her father was drunk now? Would
he blow it for her?

Mr. Riley reached into a brown bag and
offered Skip one of the bottles.

He's giving him a beer!

And much to her chagrin, Skip accepted
the bottle, twisting the cap to open it. He
took a long drink before following Mr. Riley
to the stairwell that led up to their apartment. Shannon could hear laughter echoing in the thick, salty air that hung over
the river.

Rushing into the living room, she waited
nervously until the door opened and the

two of them stepped into the apartment. Her father was smiling. Skip had a pleasant expression on his handsome face. They seemed to be getting along fine.

"Hi, Shannon," Skip said, grinning. "Sorry I'm late."

Mr. Riley offered a wink to his frowning daughter. "You got yourself a nice one here, Shannon."

Shannon grimaced. Her eyes fell on the bottle in her father's hand. The word "beer" leapt out at her.

Mr. Riley lifted the bottle. "You want one?"

"Dad!"

What was he trying to do to her?

"It's good root beer," Skip offered. "Thanks, Mr. Riley. I was thirsty."

Shannon felt herself deflating. Root beer! She had gotten all flustered over nothing.

Before anyone could utter another word, Patrick came out of his room, gaped at Skip, and said, "Oh, it's you," in a hostile tone.

Shannon froze, glaring at her younger brother with a look that said, "Knock it off, you little creep!"

Skip nodded to Patrick. "What's doing, little brother? My buds get you home okay the other day?"

"Barely," Patrick scoffed. "I thought I was going to lose my lunch. Bunch of—"

Mr. Riley's eyes narrowed. "Patrick! That's no way to speak to a guest in our home."

"Uh, sorry, Dad," Patrick replied blankly. "I have homework to do."

He darted back into his room, much to the delight of his older sister.

She found a smile for Skip. "You'll have to excuse Patrick. He's from another planet."

Skip shrugged. "Hey, I got a kid brother. I know how it is. No prob."

Shannon started toward him. "We better get going."

"Yeah," Skip replied, "I had some car trouble. Sorry I wasn't on time."

"It's all right," Shannon started. "The dance isn't over until ten-thirty."

"Just a minute!" Mr. Riley said. "Not so fast."

Shannon turned to look back at him. "Dad!" Her expression was frantic. She didn't want anyone or anything to spoil this evening.

"We have to set a curfew," he told her. "You can't stay out all night."

Skip grinned at Mr. Riley. "Just say what time you want me to have her back, sir. We'll be right on time."

Mr. Riley nodded approvingly. "Very good, young man. You seem to be of the highest caliber. Shannon, how does midnight sound? You can stay out until the stroke of twelve."

"Gee, thanks, Dad!"

"I'll have her home a few minutes early," Skip replied. "See you, Mr. Riley."

He held the door for Shannon. She went down the stairs with Skip right behind her. It was finally happening.

Skip opened the car door for her. Shannon slipped into the passenger seat of the Miata. It was such a nice little car. And everyone at Central would see her riding with Skip.

We're the perfect couple, she thought.

As Skip came around to the driver's side, Shannon peered through the windshield, gazing into the shadows of the street. For a moment, she thought she saw a boy on a bicycle, receding into the darkness. Charley! He was spying on her again!

"That little—"

Skip sat down behind the wheel. "Hey, what's wrong?"

Shannon forced a smile. "Uh, nothing."

To hell with Charley! He was only jealous. There was nothing wrong with Skip, even if the words did echo in her mind.

Katie . . . loony bin.

You don't want to end up like her!
"Skip?"

He cast a curious, puzzled look toward her. "What?"

Shannon was tongue-tied for a moment. How could she ask him if he had sent one of his girlfriends to a mental institution? Yet, it would be better than gossiping behind his back.

"Skip, I . . ."

He squinted at her. "Are you okay, Shannon?"

She sighed. "Yeah, I—I'm just in a hurry to get to the dance. Let's go."

"You got it, babe."

He turned the ignition key and the Miata roared off toward Central Academy.

She glanced sideways at Skip. His chin was held high, his brown eyes sparkled. How could he possibly be involved in anything heinous?

I have to ask, she told herself.

Skip braked the Miata to idle at a red traffic signal. "I'm ready to rock," he told her. "How about you?"

Shannon nodded absently. "Yeah, I guess."

"Are you sure that everything's okay?" Skip asked, frowning.

She took a deep breath and exhaled.

"Skip, I've heard . . . things. Things about you."

Skip's frown transformed into a look of anger. "Things?"

She nodded, looking away, avoiding his eyes. "I know they're only rumors, but I wanted to ask you myself."

"This is about Katie, isn't it?"

She glanced back in his direction, her jaw slightly agape. "Skip, I—"

"I'll tell you all about it," Skip went on. "When we get to school. I'll tell you everything."

The traffic signal turned green.

Skip floored the accelerator, screeching rubber as he flew through the narrow streets of Port City.

It was true, she thought. Everything was *true*.

But she still wouldn't believe it until she heard the whole story from Skip's own mouth.

TEN

Four boys sat in the old station wagon, watching the parking lot outside the Central Academy gymnasium. Inside the gym, the dance was underway with the majority of the student body celebrating Central's first football victory of the year. But the four boys, Skip's friends, were not going to the dance. They had other business on this cool September night.

Guy Baines put a cigarette between his fat lips and sparked a Zippo lighter. "Where are they?"

Rollie Danova glanced over from behind the wheel of the car. "They'll be here. Gimme a drag off that butt."

Guy handed him the cigarette. "You bring that booze from your father's liquor cabinet?"

Rollie grimaced. "Just can't stand it unless you have a buzz, huh?" He puffed at the cigarette and handed it back to Guy.

Guy took the cigarette, frowning at Rollie. "So, you steal that booze or what?"

Rollie looked out the window. "Under the seat."

Guy searched until he found the bottle of whiskey.

In the backseat, Peter McEvoy pounded his big knuckles into his fist. "I don't give a damn about your little substance abuse problem, Guy. Fry your brains."

Andy Rothman shifted next to Peter, sighing with boredom. "Where is he? I'm ready for some action."

"You'll have to wait," Rollie offered. "It's going to be a while. He has to take her to the dance first."

Peter slammed his hand into his fist. "I oughta kick his butt for being so late."

Andy scoffed. "You couldn't kick his butt. Skip's tougher than all of us."

Peter bristled. "Says you!"

Andy pointed a finger at him. "Lay off, you dweeb, or I'll bust a cap in your—"

"Chill out back there!" Rollie blurted out. "We don't need to be fighting. We're gonna have some fun tonight."

Guy dropped the bottle from his lips. "If that jerk ever gets here with the babe."

"Shut up, fat boy," Peter muttered. "Just suck on your baby bottle and keep your mouth closed."

Guy glanced over the backseat. "Hey, you aren't as tough as you think, McEvoy."

"How'd you like to get out of the car and try me, waste-oid? Huh? You want to—"

Rollie snapped his head around, glaring at Peter. "Shut up, McEvoy or I'll tell Skip."

Peter slumped in his seat. "Freakin' geeks."

Andy shook his head, sighing disgustedly. "What a bunch of idiots. I should shoot all of you."

Rollie smiled strangely at Andy. "Hey, remember that piece you were talking about?"

"The forty-four Magnum?" Andy replied.

Rollie nodded. "That's it."

Andy wiped the spittle from the corners of his mouth. "Man, what I wouldn't give to get my hands on that."

"How much would you give?" Rollie asked, running a hand over his head of greasy red hair.

Andy raised an eyebrow. "You gotta be joking."

Rollie nodded toward the glove compartment of the station wagon. "Guy, hand me that package in the glove."

Guy grimaced. "What?" He was already loaded.

Rollie leaned past him. "I gotta do everything myself."

Reaching into the glove compartment, Rollie took out a heavy parcel that had been wrapped in oilcloth. He handed the package back to Andy. Andy's eyes grew wide as he unfolded the cloth.

"Wow," he said in a low voice. "Where did you get this, Danova? This is great."

Rollie shrugged. "I found an open window. Be careful, though, I think it's registered."

Andy lifted the weapon into the dull glow of the streetlights that shined around Central. "Man, this is cool. I can't wait to bust off some caps."

"Save it for tonight," Rollie replied. "We may need a little persuasion later."

Peter chortled derisively. "Yeah, just like with Katie!"

Guy's face contorted into an expression of drunken rage. "Shut up, Peter. Just shut up!"

Peter started to throw a punch at Guy.

But Andy was faster. He cocked the pistol and put the bore to Peter's head. Peter froze immediately.

"You better chill," Andy said. "If you don't, your freakin' head is coming off."

"Okay, okay," Peter replied.

Rollie nodded to Andy. "Take the gun away from his head."

Andy hesitated. "Why? I'd be doing us a favor if I blew his brains out."

Rollie rolled his eyes. "It's not loaded, dweeb."

Andy's brow fretted. "Huh?"

Peter leaned back in his seat, grinning. "Not loaded. Cool. He was gonna shoot me with an unloaded gun." Peter nervously scratched the end of his flat nose.

Andy drew the gun away, laughing. "Not loaded."

Rollie also started to guffaw. "He was gonna shoot you with an unloaded gun."

The three of them chuckled so hard that the car shook. Guy was the only one who couldn't laugh. He still had nightmares about Katie. It was one of the reasons that he tried to stay high all the time.

"You guys are sick," he told them, swigging from the bottle. "Sick bunch of freaks."

They just ignored him as he swallowed another gulp of the burning liquid.

"An unloaded gun!" Peter cried.

Rollie put a finger to his mouth. "Shh, not so loud. That freak Mr. Kinsley is around. If he hears us—"

Andy waved the gun in the air. "I ain't

afraid of the assistant principal. I'll bust a cap with my unloaded gun."

The three of them laughed while Guy brooded.

After a moment, Rollie told them to shut up.

Car headlights washed over the station wagon as the Miata pulled into the parking lot.

"They're here," Rollie said.

"Time for some fun," Andy muttered.

"No," Rollie replied. "Later, after the dance. It'll all come down then."

Guy sighed and held tightly to the bottle. "Yeah, it'll all come down. Just like Katie."

ELEVEN

Skip turned the ignition key, switching off the engine of the Miata. Shannon held her breath. Had she ruined everything by asking about Katie? Why hadn't she kept her mouth shut?

I have to know the truth, she thought. *I have to!*

Skip filled his lungs and exhaled. "Katie. I really cared about that girl." His tone was more sad than angry.

Shannon felt herself relaxing a little. "Who was she?"

Skip kept his hands on the steering wheel. Would he take her home? She had blown it with him. She had destroyed their first date by bringing up a touchy subject.

"Skip, I—"

He laughed, glancing sideways at her.

"It's all right. No, really. I should've known that somebody would go slinging mud at me. Even though I didn't do anything wrong."

"Look, if you don't want to tell me . . ."

"Katie was my girlfriend," Skip started. "We went together last year. I—"

His voice cracked. He looked away for a moment. Was that a real tear that he wiped from the corner of his eye?

"She was so beautiful," Skip went on in a shaky voice. "Blond hair, blue eyes. She was a cheerleader. God, I loved that girl. I really did."

Shannon put her hand on Skip's shoulder. "What happened?"

He touched the back of her hand, sending a jolt through her body. "I—I don't know. Nobody knows. The police said she was attacked by a gang of guys. They found her out at Hampton Way Beach. She was alive. But she—she wasn't all there, if you know what I mean. I went to visit her at the hospital for a couple of months, but she just sits there, staring out the window. She doesn't talk, she barely eats. They call it a catatonic state or something like that. Shannon, if you know how many nights I couldn't sleep because of Katie." He glanced toward her again, flashing a genuine expression of remorse and agony.

Shannon smiled. "It's all right."

Charley is a fool, she thought.

Skip wasn't a monster. He was a sensitive, caring human being who had suffered a great tragedy. He needed a friend, someone to comfort him. And Shannon was just that person.

"They never found out who did it," Skip went on. "I keep hoping that she'll come out of her trance. But—"

Again, his voice broke and he lowered his head.

"Hey, it's all right," Shannon urged. "There's nothing you can do. It's not your fault."

In spite of what Charley said, she thought to herself.

Shannon would have some choice words for Charley the next time she saw him.

Skip glanced back at her, smiling weakly. "Hey, I didn't mean to bring you down."

"It's all right," she replied. "I understand. I went through a rough time recently. We all do."

"You had problems too?"

Shannon told him all about her father's recovery from alcoholism. Skip listened intently, his brow fretted. For a moment, Shannon thought she had told him too much, but at the end of her story, he shook his head and sighed.

"Wow," Skip said. "And I thought I was the only one who had it tough. At least your father is all right."

Shannon smiled when she thought about the man with a root beer in his hand. "Yeah, I'm lucky to have him back."

Forgive him, Shannon, her mother's voice whispered.

"I will," she said. Then she quickly added, "Wow, listen. You can hear the music coming out of the gym."

Skip lifted his head toward the thumping bass guitar. "Yeah. Look, if you're too bummed for the dance, we can go somewhere else."

"No way," Shannon told him. "I'm ready to rock and roll."

"Cool. Let me get the door for you."

As Skip got out of the car, Shannon caught sight of a bicycle that cut through the streaks of light from a street lamp. She tensed for a moment. But then Skip opened her door. He would protect her from Charley. Charley was the one who belonged in a loony bin!

"The evening awaits, m'lady," Skip said in a courtly tone.

Just like Cinderella, Shannon thought.

Only I won't turn into a pumpkin at midnight.

She'd turn into something much, much worse.

The four boys in the station wagon watched intently as Skip helped Shannon out of the Miata.

"If he looks over at us, the plan is on," Rollie whispered.

Guy lifted the bottle to his lips. "The plan better be on."

Peter slammed his fist into his palm. "Man, look at her. She's a choice babe."

"Just like Katie," Guy muttered.

Andy leaned forward, showing Guy the handgun. "Shut your fat mouth, you juicehead."

Guy flinched away from the cold, oily metal. "Shut up, Andy. I don't need your crap."

"Both of you shut up," Peter snapped. "Or I'll kick both your whining butts."

Rollie lifted his hand. "Wait for it. If he looks, we're on. If not—"

Suddenly, Skip turned, nodding toward the station wagon. The unsuspecting girl next to him didn't notice the gesture. But the four boys understood perfectly.

"We're on!" Rollie said.

Peter rubbed his oversized knuckles. "Yeah, she's a fox. Come on, let's go."

Rollie shook his head. "Wait until they get inside."

Guy took a long drink from the bottle. "This sucks, man. I don't think we should—"

"You don't have to go, fat boy," Andy snarled. "Stay here and drink yourself stupid."

"Bite it, gun freak," Guy replied.

Rollie pointed a finger at Guy. "Either you're in or you're out. What's it gonna be?"

Guy just sat there, not saying a word. He could still see Katie in his dreams. Once, he had even gone to the hospital to see her but he couldn't stay long enough for them to bring her into the visiting area.

"Look at him," Peter said. "He's chicken."

Andy shook his head, offering a mocking burst of laughter. "What a fat wimp."

"Are you in or out?" Rollie demanded. "Tell me now."

Guy hesitated, unable to answer.

Peter rolled his eyes. "We can't let him go."

"Why not?" Rollie asked.

"Cause he'll rat us out," Andy said. "He'll tell on us. All because of little Katie."

"Shut up!" Guy cried. "Just shut up."

"You won't rat us out, will you?" Rollie asked.

Guy shook his head. "No, I—"

"Then you're in," Rollie told him. "You can't back out now."

Guy lowered his head. "But Katie—"

"She had it coming!" Rollie snapped.

"She was a loser!" Andy rejoined.

Peter slammed his fist into his hand. "Yeah, it happened because she wanted it to happen. She couldn't take it, so she flipped out. You know that's the truth."

Rollie sighed and put his hands on the steering wheel. "You're in, Guy, whether you like it or not."

He started the car and pulled it into gear, tearing away from the campus of Central Academy.

As soon as Shannon and Skip walked into the gymnasium, every head turned in their direction. Shannon wasn't prepared for the attention that was suddenly lavished upon them. Erin came running toward them, arms extended for a friendly embrace. She hugged Shannon tightly, as if they had been pals for years.

"Hi, Shan," Erin said. "Be careful tonight."

She drew back, gazing into Shannon's eyes. What had she meant by the cryptic warning? Erin cast a strange look at Skip before she smiled at them.

Skip put his arm around Shannon's shoulder. "Hey, let's get on the dance floor while the band is rocking."

He whisked Shannon away from Erin, urging her toward the thumping rhythm of the bass guitar. Shannon quickly forgot about Erin's remark. She followed Skip, undulating to the beat, losing herself in the music. It was a magical night, an evening of rapture. The darkness had finally been lifted from her dreary life.

The band stopped for a moment between songs. Shannon smiled at Skip when the slow number started up. Skip drew her close to him, wrapping her in his strong arms. Shannon leaned her head against his chest, sighing.

"Having a good time?" he asked.

"The best," Shannon replied.

His hand stroked the back of her head. "I'm glad we got together, Shannon. I think you're a really special girl. A guy can go a long way with a girl like you."

She pulled away for a second. "What?" she asked skeptically. "What did you mean by that?"

He laughed a little. "Nothing. Just that . . . I never thought I'd find someone like you."

"Oh." She grinned. "I never thought I'd find someone like you. I—I'm so happy tonight."

"Me too."

Her head rested on his chest again.

Skip squeezed her, lowering his face to kiss her lightly on the cheek. They turned slowly on the dance floor until the music became fast again. Skip wanted to take a break, so they walked over to the refreshment table for some punch.

Shannon sipped at the sweet liquid, watching the faces that turned in her direction. Many of them were smiling. But some of the expressions had a dubious glint. A few of them were even frowning at her.

They're just jealous, she thought. *I've only been at Central for one week and I'm already popular.*

Skip took her hand. "How are you doing?"

"Fine," she replied.

"You seem a little distant," Skip told her.

She started to reply but then she saw the quick movement of a blond-haired boy. Charley Cutshawl had come into the gymnasium. He darted through the crowd, his creepy blue eyes cast in the direction of Skip and Shannon.

Shannon sighed, shaking her head.

"What's wrong?" Skip asked.

She wasn't going to let Charley ruin her evening. "Nothing. Let's dance."

They returned to the dance floor, writhing and shaking until the end of the set.

When the band took a break, Skip guided Shannon back to the refreshments.

"I'm really hungry," he told her. "How about you?"

She shrugged. "I don't know."

Skip looked at his watch. "It's almost ten o'clock. I—"

"Hello, Shannon. Having a good time?"

She glanced up to see Charley Cutshawl standing in front of her. "Charley, I—"

"Maybe Skip would let me dance with you," Charley offered. "I mean, we are friends and all."

What did Charley think he was doing?

Skip stared at Charley with a hostile look. "Take a walk, dweeb."

Charley kept staring at Shannon. "Just one dance."

Skip balled up his fist. "Just one punch, Cutshawl."

Shannon tensed, anticipating the fight. She didn't want Skip to beat up Charley, even if Charley was being a pain. Still, it made her feel good that Skip was so protective.

"Please," Shannon told them, "stop it. I don't want to dance with you, Charley."

"It's just one dance," Charley offered. "If—"

Skip grabbed the front of Charley's shirt. "Get lost, punk, or I'll tear your face off."

Charley was scared, but he still scoffed in Skip's face. "Been to see Katie lately, Skip?"

Skip bristled, baring his white teeth. "That's it, creep. You and me, outside!"

Shannon put her hand on Skip's shoulder. "No—"

Everything was turning sour in a hurry. Why did Charley have to do this? If he really was Shannon's friend, why did he want to spoil the dance for her?

"He's going to pay for this," Skip said.

"All right, what's going on here!"

The deep tone of a man's voice prompted Skip to let go of Charley. A lanky, balding man stepped between them, glancing back and forth at Skip and Charley. Harlan Kinsley, the assistant principal of Central Academy, had a stern, no-nonsense manner that froze them immediately.

Skip's going to get in trouble, Shannon thought. *It's all ruined!*

"I'm waiting for an answer!" Kinsley demanded.

Skip pointed at Charley. "This geek won't leave us alone!"

Kinsley glared at Charley. "Is that right, Cutshawl?"

"Uh, it's okay," Charley replied. "Maybe I am out of line. I'm sorry, Shannon."

He turned to walk away.

Mr. Kinsley stopped him. "I don't want any trouble out of you, Cutshawl. You either, Skip."

Skip huffed but he didn't reply.

Shannon interceded for both of them. "It's just a misunderstanding, Mr. Kinsley. I'm sorry."

Kinsley eyed the dark-haired girl with pretty green eyes. "You're new here, Ms. Riley. I just want you to know that Central Academy does not tolerate any type of unacceptable behavior. Is that clear?"

Shannon nodded. "Yes, sir."

"Very well. Enjoy the dance."

He moved off into the crowd.

Skip shook his head, frowning. "How can we enjoy the dance after that dweeb and his bull—"

Shannon put her hand on his forearm. "Maybe we should go."

He smiled suddenly. "I thought you'd never ask. Come on."

Skip took her hand, leading her out of

the gymnasium. "I've got a special place we can go," he told her.

"Where?" Shannon asked.

"Don't worry," he replied as they entered the parking lot. "You'll love it, Shannon."

"I'm sure I will," she said with a smile. But she wouldn't.

TWELVE

Skip's Miata flew along Route 1, taking the tight corners at a rate of speed that seemed almost dangerous. The windows were open allowing the night breeze to buffet Shannon's smooth face. Her long, dark hair flew in the wind as the car passed a sign announcing, HAMPTON WAY BEACH, ONE MILE. Shannon frowned when she saw the sign. Why did Hampton Way Beach sound familiar?

They found her out at Hampton Way Beach.

She was alive.

Skip had told her that Katie had been assaulted at Hampton Way Beach. Why was he bringing her here? Shannon glanced sideways at Skip. Was he thinking about the girl he had lost to mental illness?

Maybe he wanted Shannon to help him get over it. She had to be understanding, to trust him.

Damn Charley, she thought. *Why did he have to confront Skip, to bring up old memories?*

She touched Skip's shoulder. "Are you okay?"

He flinched. "Uh, yeah."

"Where are we going?"

"You'll see."

The Miata rounded a sharp curve that would take them toward a place called Lightning Point. A green and white arrow pointed the way. Suddenly Shannon could smell the salt air, could hear the waves crashing against a rocky beach.

In her mind's eye, she saw Skip taking her for a walk along a romantic shore. The sky was clear with stars streaking the dark firmament. They'd hold hands, share their first kiss. She'd erase all the bad memories of his other girlfriends. Shannon would be the only one in his thoughts.

Skip turned away from the beach, taking a narrow road into the shadows of a thinly wooded coastal plain. Shannon kept her eyes wide open, wondering why they weren't stopping along the seashore route. If they were supposed to walk along the ocean, why had they gone in the opposite direction?

"Skip—"

"Hold your water, Shannon," he snapped back at her without warning. "You're gonna have a good time tonight, okay!"

She didn't like the imposing tone of his voice. And the look on his face now seemed hostile. What had happened to change him so abruptly?

"Skip, please . . . I want to go home."

"Shut up, Shannon. Just shut up."

Her own expression grew angry. "You can't talk to me like that, Skip."

He chortled at her. "I can do whatever I want, babe. And there's not a thing you can do to stop me."

The Miata bounced on the narrow path, jostling Shannon in the passenger seat. The car burst through the coastal vegetation, emerging in a clearing. Headlight beams washed over the station wagon and the figures of four boys who leaned against the wall of a dilapidated cedar-shingled shack. Skip braked the vehicle, skidding to a halt, switching off the engine. The headlights went out and the boys disappeared for a moment.

"Get out of the car, Shannon," Skip said in a gruff voice. "Now."

She shook her head. "No, Skip. I want

you to take me home. Turn the car around."

He laughed in her face. "No way, babe. The party is just starting. Now get out of the car!"

"No!" She folded her arms. "Take me home or I'll—"

Skip opened his car door, climbing out. He came toward Shannon in the darkness. Her anger quickly changed into fear. She felt paralyzed as he threw open the door of the passenger side.

"Get out of the car, you little tease!"

Her voice trembled. "No."

Skip grabbed her, trying to yank her from the Miata. Shannon grabbed the steering wheel, bracing herself. But he was too strong. She flew out of the car and landed with a dull thud on the moist ground.

"Oh yeah," Skip said, his chest heaving. "Gonna have some big fun tonight."

"No," Shannon muttered, "please—"

She tried to stand up. Skip pushed her down into the dirt again. Shannon's face smashed against soft, black soil that tasted slightly salty.

"You're gonna do what you're told," Skip snarled. "Don't get any ideas about running away. It's not gonna happen."

Shannon lifted her head toward the

sounds of approaching voices. The others were coming to join Skip. What did they have in mind? Her body shuddered. She knew what they wanted. And she was powerless against five of them.

"Hey, Skip," Rollie Danova called, "what took you so long?"

Shannon saw his face in the flame of a matchstick as he lit a cigarette. The others stood beside him.

Peter slammed his fist into his palm. "If she gives us any trouble, I'll knock her around a little."

A pistol hammer clicked in Andy's hand. "Hey, you be a good girl or I might have to use this."

Guy had drank half the whiskey, but he still kept at the bottle. "Poor kid."

Skip turned to glare at him. "What's with you?"

Guy looked away, swigging from the bottle.

Rollie laughed as he dragged from the cigarette. "He's having an attack of conscience."

"Yeah," Peter said, "I oughta kick his ass."

"Maybe I'll shoot him," Andy offered.

Skip shook his head. "Man, he's a wimp."

Shannon lay there, listening to them, wondering how they could even think of doing something like this. Charley had been right all along. And she remembered Erin's cryptic admonition. Had these boys done something similar to Erin? To other girls? The girl named Katie had been sent away. How could Skip do something like this to his own girlfriend?

"Who's going first?" Andy asked.

Skip's narrow eyes focused on the boy who held the gun. "I'm first, you jerk. I did all the work to get her here."

"I'm not gonna do it," Guy said drunkenly. "You guys can all go to hell."

Rollie offered a weird grin. "Wait a minute. Let Guy go first. Make him do it. That way he can't get righteous later."

Skip turned on Guy. "Righteous? You think he's gonna blab? Rat us out?"

Peter pushed at Guy. "He's been talking like that."

Skip's mouth opened slightly in a devilish smirk. "Okay, Guy's going first."

"No way!"

They're arguing, she thought. *They're fighting over me like dogs with a scrap of meat.*

She had to get to her feet, to run away from them. She couldn't just lie down and take it. She had to escape.

Skip grabbed Guy and pushed him against the car, holding a fist in his face.

"You're gonna do it, waste-boy. And you aren't gonna tell anyone. Are you?"

"Shut up, Skip!" Guy slurred. "You can't—"

Skip slapped him with a flat hand.

Guy began to whimper.

"Freakin' wimp!"

As they argued among themselves, Shannon became aware that they were no longer paying attention to her. If she could get to her feet, she might be able to run away from them. She'd have to be fast. If only her legs felt like something other than concrete posts. There was no spring in her body, no energy. Yet, she had to try if she wanted to escape.

Get off the ground, she told herself. *Run. You don't want to end up like Katie!*

Shannon pushed herself out of the dirt with her arms. She managed to balance on her wobbly legs. As she stood up, the boys' eyes focused on her.

"Hey, look at this," Rollie said, exhaling a puff of smoke. "She's ready!"

Shannon wheeled on her feet, starting away from them as fast as her legs would carry her.

"Get her!" Skip cried.

I won't let them catch me.

She bolted from the road, entering the wooded area. Rough fingers of brush stung

her face. She tripped suddenly, falling into
a puddle of brackish water. She had found
the edge of a marsh. And in the darkness,
she had no idea which way to turn.

Voices filled the night air.

"She went in the woods!"

"Circle around!"

"Freakin' tease!"

"You see her?"

"No!"

"Somebody get a flashlight!"

Shannon had to keep going. She ran
blindly through the marsh, her feet splash-
ing in shallow water. The mud became
softer, thicker. After a few more steps, she
was knee-deep in mire.

How was she going to get away from
them?

Their voices echoed in the sea air.

"See her?"

"Not yet!"

"She can't get far."

I can *get far*, Shannon thought.

The muck tugged at her, trying to pull
her into the earth. Turning parallel to the
edge of the marsh, Shannon began to
trudge through the sticky ooze, hoping to
find drier ground. Finally the earth
seemed to harden a little, allowing her to
move quicker. She thought she was run-

ning away from them. The voices were
definitely behind her.

"You get that flashlight?"

"Yeah, here it is."

"Shine it in the marsh."

The beam of light swung through the
trees but it didn't hit Shannon. She knew
she could make it. She *had* to make it.
Even if the swamp didn't want her to break
free.

"I heard her!"

"Over there."

"I'll circle back."

She could hear them running. Eventually they'd come into the marsh after her.
She had to get to the other side.

When she broke free of the wild vegetation, Shannon thought she had escaped.
But then she looked up to see the cedar-
shingled shack. She had circled back to the
clearing! The Miata sat a few feet away,
parked on the narrow road.

"No!"

She spun toward the marsh again but
Skip was there, slapping her with the flat
of his hand. When he hit her, Shannon fell
to the ground again. Her ears rang from
the blow. She felt dizzy, as if she was going
to pass out.

Skip hovered against the sky, glaring
down at her. "I got her! She's over here!"

Shannon tried to rise again. Skip grabbed her by the hair, dragging her to the center of the clearing. The other boys appeared to form a circle around her.

"Nice try, babe," Skip said. "You almost missed the fun."

He let go of her hair, dropping her into the dirt again.

"Now," Rollie said, "where were we?"

Peter laughed maniacally. "It's Guy's turn to party."

"Yeah," Rollie rejoined. "Guy's the guy."

Andy bent down with the pistol, grabbing Shannon's face, putting the barrel of the gun in her ear. "Any more trouble from you, slut, and I'll scatter your brains all over the county."

Shannon closed her eyes, groaning, muttering under her breath, begging for mercy. But they didn't hear her. They were intent on forcing Guy to be the first one to victimize her.

"She's going in the shed," Skip told him. "And you're going with her, Baines. You hear me?"

Guy still held the liquor bottle in his hand. "Okay," he said reluctantly. "But I'm taking my booze with me."

"That's right," Peter cackled, "take your bottle with you. You little wussy baby!"

Skip nodded toward the cedar-shingled

shack. "Come on. Let's get her inside. Then it happens."

"Just like Katie," Guy muttered.

They picked her up, carrying her across the clearing, dropping her on the floor of the shack. Skip shoved Guy inside with her. He closed the door, leaving them alone.

"Call us when you're finished!" Skip yelled.

Shannon could hear the others laughing. She expected Guy to pounce on her like a jungle animal. Instead, he bent down and gently touched her face.

"Are you okay?" he whispered.

Shannon tried to crawl away from him. "Leave me alone."

"It'll be all right," he said. "I'm not going to do anything to you. Okay?"

He took a long drink from the bottle.

Shannon could not see his face in the shadows, but she could make out his silhouette. "Save me from them," she pleaded.

He shook his head. "I can't."

"But they're going to hurt me!"

"I know. But there's nothing I can do about it."

Another shudder played through Shannon's body. "It's Katie, isn't it? You feel bad about her."

Guy exhaled, shaking his head. "I dream about her."

"Then help me!"

"I can't."

Shannon had to exploit his weakness. But how? She heard the clinking of the bottle as it tapped the floor of the shack.

"Is there anything left to drink?" she asked.

"Why?"

"I—if they're going to do something to me, it might help me if I had something to drink."

He sighed again. "Sure, here—"

As soon as the bottle touched her hand, Shannon gripped it tightly, swinging it hard into Guy's head. He made a grunting sound but he didn't go down. Shannon hit him again, and again. Finally, he dropped to the floor of the shack, convulsing as blood dripped from his skull.

Shannon scuffled to her feet. She had to get out of the shack. But how? They were guarding the door. She could hear them outside. She'd never get past them.

"Hey, how you doin' in there, Guy?"

"Having fun yet?"

"Hey, I don't hear nothin'. Let's check it out."

"Nah, leave them alone. He'll come out when he's done."

Shannon staggered in the darkness, looking for a way out. Her feet hit some loose floorboards. She bent down, pulling at the boards. They came up easily, allowing her to ease down under the floor. The crawl space was dark and wet. For a moment, she considered the idea of hiding under the shack. No, they'd eventually come to see what had happened to their friend. They'd find her then.

Taking a deep breath, Shannon lowered her head and started to crawl. It was slippery and cold beneath the shack. Something slithered out from under her as she moved slowly toward a wafting breeze. After a few minutes, she emerged behind the shed, free but still frightened. How long would it take for them to realize what had happened? And where would she go? Back into the marsh?

Shannon flinched when a hand fell on her shoulder. She started to cry out but a second hand closed on her mouth, preventing her from uttering a sound. They had captured her again.

"It's me," a familiar voice whispered. "And I'm going to get you out of here!"

Charley!

He removed his hand from her mouth.

"How?" she whispered. "How did you—"

"I knew where Skip was taking you,"

Charley said softly. "Come on, let's get out of here."

Taking her hand, Charley led her back toward the marsh. But he knew a different path that took them to the highway. His mountain bike had been stashed in the bushes.

"You can sit on the handlebars," he told her.

"Charley, I—"

"Just get on," he said. "We have to make it back to town before they catch us."

Shannon stiffened. "Can we make it before they—"

"Just get on!"

Shannon climbed onto the handlebars. Charley began to pedal toward town. The road was dark and deserted until the headlights appeared behind them.

"It's Skip!" Shannon cried.

Charley looked back over his shoulder. "Maybe not."

"I know it," Shannon replied. "We have to hide."

Charley pulled off to the side of the road. They stashed the bike in the brush and dropped to their stomachs. Sure enough, the Miata passed them. Charley started to stand up. Shannon pulled yanked him down again.

"What?" he asked.

"Wait for the station wagon."

A minute passed before the station wagon roared by them. Shannon could see Rollie, Peter, and Andy. Guy was probably lying in back. Had she really escaped them?

"I hate them," she muttered.

Charley shook his head. "I tried to warn you."

"I know. I'm sorry."

"You're sorry! You're lucky they didn't kill you!"

"I know."

He sighed. "Wow, you're all dirty. Come on, we have to get to a phone to call your father."

"No," Shannon replied.

"No?"

"Take me into Port City," Shannon replied. "I want to go to the police."

"Now you're talking," Charley replied. "We'll fix those creeps for good!"

They boarded the mountain bike, pedaling for Port City, their eyes aware of every headlight that passed.

Shannon's father arrived at the police station while she was telling her story to Victor Danridge, the chief of police for Port City. Mr. Riley gawked at his daughter's dirty face. His body trembled as he em-

braced her. Shannon finished her grue-
some tale and then repeated it for the
police chief. Charley backed her up on
some of the details.

"He's done this to more than one girl,"
Charley offered. "His old girlfriend Katie is
in the loony bin."

Danridge, a steely-eyed man in a dark
suit, glared at Charley. "Stick to the facts,
Mr. Cutshawl."

Mr. Riley glared at the law officer. "What
are you going to do about this?"

Dandridge leaned forward on his desk.
"I'm going to round up these boys and hear
their side of the story. If you'd like to wait,
you can go ahead and file a complaint."

"You're damned right I'm going to file a
complaint!" Mr. Riley replied. "Point me in
the right direction."

While her father filled out the paper-
work, Shannon cleaned up in one of the
station bathrooms. Charley then sat with
her in the waiting area, holding her hand.
They didn't say much to each other. Shannon felt badly about not believing Charley.
She had to tell him that she should've
listened.

They both looked up when they heard
the laughter of the five boys who were
striding toward Danridge's office. Skip led
the way. He nodded toward Shannon when

he saw her, pretending that nothing was wrong as an officer opened the door.

"I had a great time at the dance," he said. "See you in school on Monday."

Shannon glared at him. "You're slime, Skip. Slime!"

"Hey, what'd I do?" Skip replied.

"Yeah," Rollie offered. "What'd he do?"

Laughing derisively, the five of them disappeared into the office. Guy was the last to go in. He cast a weird look in Shannon's direction. He wore a bandage on the side of his head where she had hit him. Would Guy tell the truth? Or would he go along with his friends?

It seemed like forever to Shannon before the boys emerged from the office, still smiling and laughing. They walked past Shannon and Charley, never turning to look at them. Chief Danridge appeared at the door of his office, motioning for Mr. Riley to come in. Mr. Riley stormed out a few minutes later, huffing and puffing.

According to Chief Danridge, the boys had an alibi to clear them of Shannon's accusations. Skip had told him that he dropped Shannon at her house after the dance. Then he went out with his buddies, driving around for the rest of the evening. His four cohorts corroborated the story. Shannon and Charley were outnumbered,

five to two. Danridge had to believe Skip
and his friends, as a jury would if the case
went to trial.

Danridge was sorry. He couldn't do a
thing to help Shannon. He speculated that
there wouldn't be any more trouble. It had
simply been a misunderstanding.

Of course, Shannon knew that Chief
Danridge was wrong.

Dead wrong.

THIRTEEN

The next Monday after the incident at the beach, Mr. Riley wanted Shannon to stay out of school. But Shannon refused to miss classes. She would not get behind in her schoolwork. Nor would she avoid Skip and his friends. Shannon intended to look them in their hateful eyes, condemning them for what they had done.

That morning, Charley met her on the sidewalk, riding his bike next to Shannon. They didn't say much, though Shannon treated him like a friend. Charley had saved her from Skip's treachery. She knew the only way she could repay Charley was to accept him now as a friend, nothing more, a fate that Charley seemed to acknowledge. She could still see the longing in his eyes, however. Charley had a crush on her.

Patrick walked with them, aware that something had happened to his sister, though he was sketchy on the facts. Shannon and Mr. Riley had chosen to leave out the gory details of the unfortunate Saturday night. Patrick seemed satisfied to be kept in the dark about everything, as he had his own agenda at Central Academy.

When they arrived on the Central campus, Shannon was nervous, expecting the worst from Skip and his cohorts. Charley stayed near her until the bell rang for homeroom. As soon as he left her alone in the hallway, Shannon lifted her head to see Skip coming straight at her in the corridor.

She froze against the wall of lockers, expecting some sort of retaliation in the form of a rude comment or a cutting slur. But Skip walked on past, ignoring her, talking to some other girl who might end up as his next victim. Shannon considered seeking out the girl, to tell her all about Skip. She finally decided that no one would believe her, so she had better keep quiet. What was done was done. There was no need to give Skip a reason to come after her again.

All morning, she kept watching and waiting for the other four boys to approach her. But they also ignored her. Guy still wore a bandage on his head where Shannon had hit him. As Shannon passed him in the hallway, Guy glanced sideways at her for a moment. But when their eyes met, he kept walking.

In her fourth period class, Shannon held her breath, waiting for Skip to enter the room. He strode in with a cocky smile on his face. He acted like Shannon wasn't even there. She hated him. She longed for revenge. But how?

After class, they took their separate routes to the cafeteria. Charley met Shannon at the lunch line and they went through with their trays. When they finally found a couple of empty seats, they slid down into chairs on opposite sides of the table.

"Any trouble?" Charley asked.

Shannon shook her head. "Not so far."

Charley sighed. "I don't think they'll try anything. Not yet, anyway. It's too soon after they saw the police chief."

Shannon stared at her lunch tray, unable to eat. "I know I have to let it go, Charley, but I keep thinking about the way they treated me. I hate them."

"So do I," Charley replied. "So do I."

"I think they're going to leave me alone now," Shannon offered.

"I hope so."

They were quiet until a loud, raucous burst of laughter filled the lunchroom. Shannon lifted her eyes to see Skip and the other four boys sitting at a table a few rows down from her and Charley. For a brief instant, Shannon met a cold, hard gaze of the handsome boy. He no longer made her heart miss a beat. Skip stared right at her, unrepentant, before he glanced away.

I hate him, Shannon thought.

"Don't look at him," Charley said.

"I won't," she replied.

The rest of the day was like a dull, waking nightmare. Shannon went through the motions but she could barely concentrate in her classes. After the sound of the final bell, she met Patrick and Charley at Patrick's locker. Her younger brother told her he was staying late at the library to work on a report. Shannon replied that he had better not stay too long. Patrick waved her off, saying that he would walk home with one of his new friends, a pretty girl who waited at the other end of the hall.

Shannon left the school grounds with Charley beside her. All the way back to the waterfront, she kept expecting Skip and his thugs to jump out of the afternoon shadows. But the only disturbance in Port City was a cool breeze that stirred the leaves in the trees. The elms and maples were already starting to show tinges of red and gold, promising a colorful autumn.

Charley saw her to the stairwell that led up to the apartment. Shannon said good-bye, even though she could tell that he wanted to come up. She climbed the stairs in a gloomy funk that turned to terror when she entered the apartment.

Skip leapt from behind the door, grabbing her, pushing her down into the couch. "Hi there, you little tease. Glad to see me?"

She wanted to cry out but his hand covered her mouth.

"Oh, don't worry," Skip told her. "I'm not gonna hurt *you*. No, I just wanted to say hello. To tell you how much I missed you. Too bad you couldn't hang around Saturday night. We could've had some real fun."

She trembled beneath his weight, wondering if he would kill her.

Suddenly Skip raised up, freeing her. "So long, Princess. It's been real." He ran out of the apartment, clomping down the stairs before she could scream.

I'm not gonna hurt you.

What had he meant by that? Shannon sat on the couch for nearly an hour, unable to move as she tried to compose herself. The phone rang next to her, making her jump.

"Hello?"

It was her father. He told her to come quickly. Patrick was in the Port City community hospital. He had fallen from the second story of the Central Academy library. The girl with whom he had been studying could not explain what Patrick had been doing up there. Nor could she shed any light on who or what had caused his fall.

But Shannon knew.

The name formed on her lips. "Skip."

No! His *friends* were responsible, Shannon was sure of it.

She ran all the way to the hospital, stopping a couple of times to ask directions. When she arrived at the intensive care unit, Mr. Riley met her in the hall. He was frantic, almost delirious. He led Shannon to the window where she could look in on her brother.

The doctors told them that Patrick had suffered severe brain damage in the fall. He was in a coma. Her little brother might never wake up. And even if he did, he would never be the same.

Mr. Riley broke down, sobbing with his face in his hands.

But Shannon only stared coldly at the lifeless form.

I'm going to kill them, she thought. *I'm*

*going to kill them all. They won't get away
with this.*

This time, there was no inner voice to
cajole her toward tolerance or forgiveness.

Shannon wanted Skip and his friends to
die.

And she would think of a way to get even
with them.

Even if it took forever!

FOURTEEN

Shannon sat opposite the wheelchair, gazing at her younger brother. Patrick wore a foolish grin on his face. He wasn't smiling, however. He was catatonic: alive and conscious, but not really there.

Shannon touched his hand. "Patrick? We really missed you at Christmas. We really . . ." Her voice trailed off.

Christmas and New Year's had been almost impossible without Patrick there. Their father was having a tough time. Mr. Riley had been attending workshops and support groups to try to keep from returning to his alcoholic ways. So far he had been succcooful, but Shannon wasn't sure he would make it. She wasn't sure that she would be able to keep *herself* together.

She let go of Patrick's hand. "Good-bye, Patrick. I'll see you next week."

She got up, heading for a corridor that smelled of antiseptic. Every day had been a struggle, even after Patrick had awakened from the coma. Her father hadn't been able to afford to put Patrick in a nursing home, so he had gone to the state hospital on the outskirts of Port City. Shannon hated visiting the run-down, second-rate facility, but she was not going to give up on her brother despite the predictions of the doctors that he would never return to his former self.

As Shannon left the red brick building, a cold, stiff wind buffeted her face. January snow lay on the ground, piled in high drifts where snowplows and snowblowers had cleared the streets and walkways. Shannon drew her collar tightly around her neck. It was going to be a long wait for the bus. She hurried to the bus stop, cowering in a corner of the shelter to stay out of the wind.

"Hey, Shannon!"

A car horn honked. She turned to see a Lincoln Town Car pulling up next to the curb. The window was down on the passenger side. Charley Cutshawl looked out at her.

"Charley, what are you doing here?"

He waved at her. "Get in. Dad let me have the car. I knew you'd be here."

Shannon surely wasn't going to turn down a chance to get out of the cold. Climbing in, she immediately flipped the button that would raise the power window. She pressed her hands against the heating vents for warmth.

"Thanks," she muttered.

"No problem. I know you always come here on Sunday. Your Dad couldn't make it, huh?"

She shivered. "He can't take it anymore. I'm afraid he's going to start drinking again."

Charley sighed. He expected Shannon to cry, but there were no more tears inside her.

Shannon gazed out at the drifts of snow. Her thoughts of revenge had subsided a little. Not because she had abandoned the idea of getting even. She just knew that, deep inside her, she wasn't the kind of person who could hurt anyone. In her mind, she could torture Skip and his friends, visit heinous, horrible fates upon them. But in reality, she just couldn't do it.

"Want to go for a burger?" Charley asked. "I'm buying."

She nodded. "Sure, why not?"

Charley frowned. "Damn it all. Why did

Skip have to do this? What's his freakin' problem anyway?"

"I don't know."

"I wish they were dead," Charley went on. "I wish they'd all commit suicide. That'd be a problem taking care of itself."

Shannon hesitated and then her eyes grew wide. *A problem taking care of itself.*

Shannon pointed straight ahead. "Take me home."

Charley grimaced, disappointed that she was suddenly canceling an almost date. "Home. But—"

"I want you to come home with me," Shannon told him. "I'm going to need your help, Charley."

"My help?"

A problem taking care of itself.

"Just take me home, Charley. I'll explain everything."

Charley had inadvertently given her the answer. Now all she had to do was work out the details. And if everything went right, Shannon could avenge her brother's plight without getting her hands dirty.

Shannon and Charley sat in the Lincoln, watching the house across the street. They had come to Washington Avenue in Prescott Estates, the fancy neighborhood where Andy Rothman lived with his parents. Next to Charley lay the cellular phone that he had borrowed from his father who used the phone in his real estate business.

Charley sighed, glancing at the clock on the dashboard. "It's going to be dark in another half hour," he told Shannon. "Maybe we should—"

Shannon raised her hands. "Shh, look! They're leaving."

Andy and his parents came out of the old Victorian house, heading for the car in the driveway. Shannon figured Andy was the best place to start. She knew his weakness. So did Charley.

"He's a gun freak Shannon! If he catches us in his house—"

She turned to glare at Charley. "Look, if you don't want to help me, then I'll do it myself."

Charley shook his head. "No, I'll help."

He thought Shannon's plan was crazy. It had taken them almost two weeks to figure everything. But now they were ready to set the scheme in motion.

No turning back.

If Charley hadn't been totally in love with Shannon he wouldn't have gone along with it.

Shannon watched as the car pulled away

with Andy and his parents. Andy sat in the backseat, scowling. He was probably mad that he had to go somewhere with his mother and father. He wanted to be with Skip and his friends, taking advantage of some hapless female.

She opened her door. "Come on."

"Shannon!"

"Just do it!"

They got out, crossing the street.

Shannon stopped on the sidewalk. "I saw them lock the front door. We'll have to try the back."

Charley looked up and down the street. "What if somebody sees us?"

"Then we'll say we're looking for Andy. Come on."

They trudged around to the back door with Charley lamenting the footprints that they left in the snow. Shannon clomped up the back steps, trying the door. It was open. She entered the house, moving into a kitchen that had been decorated in a country style.

"We have to find his room," Shannon whispered.

"What if he doesn't keep his guns there?" Charley offered.

Shannon started forward without a reply. The living room of the house was gorgeous, hardly the kind of dwelling that

belonged to a thug like Andy. She turned
toward a set of stairs that led to the second
story. Despite Charley's warnings that the
Rothmans might return, Shannon began to
climb. Charley followed her, thinking that
he was crazy for being in love with this
madwoman.

"Shannon!"

"Look, I bet this is Andy's room."

She pushed open a door that led them
into the shadows of Andy's bedroom. There
were pictures and posters of guns on the
walls. The room was a mess, littered with
candy wrappers, soda bottles, and half-
eaten sandwiches.

"What a porker," Charley muttered.

"Come on, we have to find the guns."

They began searching the drawers and
closets, coming up empty.

"Maybe he doesn't keep them here,"
Charley offered.

Shannon pointed to the bed. "Look under
there."

Charley dropped to the floor, reaching
under the bed. "I don't—whoa, wait a
minute!"

Charley pulled a leather sports bag from
beneath the box spring. It was heavy, laden
with iron. They unzipped the bag to find a
cache of handguns. There was also a small
photo album.

Shannon opened the album to find pictures of girls. "Look, that girl Katie. And these others—"

"Victims," Charley said. "The girls that Skip lured into his trap. Look, there's Erin."

"She never told anyone," Shannon said. "And if you hadn't saved me, Charley, I'd be in there. My picture would . . ."

She shivered. Charley put his arm around her shoulder. Suddenly, she turned to kiss him, pressing her lips to his mouth. When she drew back, Charley was blushing.

"Shannon—"

"Don't say anything," she told him. "Just—Charley, what was that? Listen!"

Charley cocked his head. "I don't hear anything."

Shannon had heard it clearly. A car door had slammed in the Rothman's driveway. Someone walked up the front steps.

They heard Andy's voice bellowing in the cold air. "Oh yeah! Well, I didn't want to go anyway!"

Andy slammed the front door. Shannon and Charley looked at each other. He was back. And he'd be coming up to his room to play with his guns.

Shannon pointed to the window. Charley grimaced as if to say, "We're on the second floor." Shannon hurried to the casement, opening the window. She waved for Charley to follow her. Charley lugged the bag of guns to the opening.

"Throw them out," Shannon whispered. "Now! Before he comes up here. Go on!"

Charley flung the bag into the snow below them. "What now?"

"We're next," Shannon replied.

Easing through the open window, she lowered her legs and then let her body hang from the casement. She dangled for a moment before releasing her grip. Shannon's stomach floated inside her for the brief instant of the drop. But then she hit the snow drift, landing harmlessly in the soft, white mound.

Charley gazed down with a fearful expression on his face. Shannon waved frantically for him to hurry. Andy's footsteps were echoing from the stairs that led to the second story. Repeating Shannon's daredevil feat, Charley hung from the casement and then dropped into the snow drift.

"Let's get out of here," he whispered.

Shannon hunkered in the growing shadows. "Wait a minute."

"But he's in his room!"

She pointed to the street where the

Rothmans were pulling away from the house.

"Now!"

They ran through the yard as fast as the deep snow would let them. Shannon did not glance back because she was afraid that Andy would look out his window and see them. As soon as they were inside the car, she glanced back at the second story. The window was still open. Shannon flinched when it dropped down, slamming shut.

"Peel out of here," she told Charley. "Head for Peter's."

"Shannon—"

"Go, before Andy sees the car and realizes that it's us."

Charley cranked up the engine and drove away from Prescott Estates. Shannon told him the address for Peter's house. He lived on Taylor Street in Pitney Docks, only a few blocks away from Shannon. As they drove through the streets, the sky grew darker and the street lamps were turned on.

"This is crazy," Charley told her.

"I don't care," Shannon replied. "We have to do it. It's the only way."

A problem taking care of itself.

"We can't turn back now," Shannon muttered under her breath.

The plan was in motion.
The die had been cast.
It has to work, she told herself.
But even if it didn't, it was too late for
them to stop.

FIFTEEN

Charley eased the big car next to the curb and shut off the engine. Shannon gazed toward the dilapidated townhouse on the other side of Taylor Street. The place was dark, empty.

Perfect. So far.

Charley nodded toward the bag of guns sitting between them. "I think those pictures are enough evidence for the police. Why don't we just—"

Shannon turned to glare at him. "Right, we stroll into the police station with an album full of pictures. Some evidence."

"What about Erin? Maybe she'd come forward."

Shannon shook her head. "No way. If she was going to talk, she would've done it already."

They were silent for a moment, both gazing in the direction of Peter McEvoy's dwelling.

Charley sighed. "You kissed me back there."

"I know," Shannon replied. "That was for saving me."

"I love you, Shannon. I'm totally in love with you."

"Can we talk about this later?"

"We don't have to talk about it at all if you're not in love with me, Shannon."

She grabbed the heavy bag and opened the car door. "I have to do this, Charley. Are you coming with me?"

He reached for the door handle. "Yes. I just hope Peter doesn't catch us."

They crossed Taylor Street under the glow of the street lamps. There were no signs of life in the run-down townhouse. Shannon and Charley went around to the back door but Shannon stopped on the porch, gazing into the tiny backyard.

"Look," she whispered. "A shed."

Charley grimaced. "So what?"

"Put the guns there," Shannon offered. "That way we don't have to go inside."

Charley was sweating even in the cold air. "Man, this is crazy. Really dim."

"Yeah, but it's going to work," Shannon replied.

She hurried to the rickety shed, which was unlocked. Easing into the seedy structure, she found a hiding place for the bag behind a stack of firewood. It had to look good, as if Peter had stashed the guns himself.

Shannon came out to find Charley standing in the snow. "Let's get back to the car."

"You don't have to tell me twice," Charley replied.

They ran through the icy white cover, their breaths fogging the night air. When they were inside the Lincoln, Charley started the engine and cranked up the heater. Shannon peered at the townhouse, waiting for Peter to come home.

"Do you have the phone ready?" Shannon asked.

Charley nodded. "Shannon, I don't know about this. Someone could get hurt."

"I hope so," Shannon replied.

They waited for nearly an hour before the station wagon pulled up in front of Peter's house. Rollie Danova was at the wheel. Shannon and Charley ducked low in the seat, waiting for Rollie to leave. As soon as the station wagon drove away, they raised their heads, watching Peter McEvoy enter through the front door.

"Do it," Shannon said. "And don't forget to disguise your voice."

"Shannon—"

"Do it, or hand the phone to me."

Charley picked up the cellular phone, dialing Andy's number. Andy answered on the second ring. Charley hesitated, his pulse racing, sweat dripping from his cheeks.

"Hello?" Andy demanded. "Who is this?"

Charley's lips were trembling but he managed to get it out. "Where are your guns, Andy?" he asked in a spooky voice.

Hesitation from the gun freak. "You took them!"

"No, it was Peter," Charley went on. "He took them."

"Peter? Peter McEvoy?"

"He knows all about you and he's going to tell on you," Charley said. "He has your photo album. He's going to talk Erin into testifying against you. You're going to take the fall for Skip and the others."

"You're crazy!"

"Peter has your guns, Andy. They're hidden in his woodshed, behind his house."

"No way, he'd never—"

"If you don't believe me, take a look for yourself."

"Wait a minute—"

Charley hung up the phone, drawing a

deep breath. "Man, my heart is pounding like a jackhammer."

Shannon touched his trembling hand. "I know. Mine too. You did great."

"What now?" he asked.

Shannon exhaled. "We wait."

They didn't have to wait long.

Andy jogged up the sidewalk, rushing toward Peter's house. He stopped for a moment, peering toward the woodshed in the backyard. He glanced at the house before turning in the direction of the shed. Cautiously, he tiptoed through the snow. He was going to check behind the woodpile before he confronted Peter.

"There he goes," Shannon said.

Charley bit his lip. "Man, I hope he—"

Andy came bursting out of the woodshed, racing for the back door. He didn't even knock. After few moments, Shannon and Charley could see two silhouettes in the window.

Shannon reached for the door handle. "I've got to get closer."

Charley's eyes grew wide. "What?"

"I want to hear what's going on!"

"Shannon, don't—"

But it was too late. She had already gotten out and slammed the door. Charley watched her cross the street. He had to follow her. He loved her too much to let her go alone.

As they slid next to the downstairs window, they could hear the boys arguing with each other.

"I didn't take your guns!" Peter snapped.

"Then what were they doing in your woodshed?" Andy demanded.

"I don't know. It's a frame-up."

"You're lying, McEvoy. You're gonna turn me in. All of you. You're gonna finger *me* for what we did to those girls. Erin is gonna talk. And you're gonna let *me* take the fall."

"Get your butt outta here now, Rothman, or I'm gonna take your face off. You hear me? Beat it!"

Shannon cringed against the wall. She had been counting on Peter's hateful temper. He was losing it now.

"Screw you!" Andy cried. "I'm not taking the rap for something we all did. I—ow—"

Peter had taken a swing at him. Shannon heard scuffling for a few minutes. Then it really turned ugly.

"What are you doing with that gun?" she heard Peter say.

"I'm not going down for you jerks," Andy replied.

"Put the piece away, Rothman. If you don't, you'll be sorry."

"You're the one who's going to be sorry."

Shannon pointed to the car. "Let's get out of here," she whispered, "Hurry!"

They ran across the street, climbing into the Lincoln.

Shannon gazed back at the house, watching as the two figures struggled in the window. She saw the flash of the gun muzzle, heard the muffled report of the weapon. One of the figures fell to the floor. But which one?

After a long wait, Andy slipped through the front door, rushing down the steps. He slipped on the ice and fell on the sidewalk. Scuffling to his feet, he hurried away from the house carrying the black bag with him. Shannon and Charley ducked down until he disappeared around the corner.

"I wonder if anyone heard the shot besides us?" Charley wondered aloud.

"I don't care," Shannon replied.

"Maybe we should go to the police?"

She shook her head. "No. We still have work to do. Take me back to Andy's place."

"Shannon . . . Peter might be dead."

"I know. Now, take me to Andy's house."

As Charley pulled the Lincoln into gear, he wondered what he had gotten himself into. Shannon was turning Skip's friends against each other. He wondered how she could do it, until he thought of Patrick in the state hospital. Maybe Peter and Andy had it coming. Maybe they were just getting what they deserved.

They beat Andy back to Prescott Estates. Shannon told Charley to park next to the curb. They waited until Andy got home. As soon as he was inside, Shannon pointed to the cellular phone.

"Give it to me," she said.

Charley sighed. "Shannon—"

"Like I said, if you don't want to go through with it—"

He handed her the phone. She dialed Andy's number. It rang at least ten times before he picked up inside.

"Hello?"

Shannon lowered her voice to a ghostly baritone. "It was Rollie," she told him. "Rollie knows you killed Peter. He's going to turn you in to the police."

"Who the hell is this?" Andy cried.

"It's Katie."

"Katie!"

"Rollie is the one," she repeated. "He knows you shot Peter. He's going to the police tonight."

"I'll bust a cap in him, just like I did Peter."

"Hurry," Shannon said. "Before Rollie gets to the police."

She switched off the cellular phone.

"You think he's going to do it?" Charley wondered aloud.

Shannon nodded toward the front door. "There he goes."

Andy bolted from the house, carrying something in his right hand. He stopped on the sidewalk, tucking the gun into his belt. Closing his coat over the weapon, he started walking again.

"Do you want to follow him?" Charley asked.

Shannon shook her head. "No. Take me home."

Charley put the car into gear again. "Man, this is wild."

He drove through the narrow streets of Port City, making for the waterfront. When he pulled in front of Shannon's apartment building, he said good night to Shannon. She put her hand on his forearm and asked him to come up.

They climbed the stairs to the apartment. Mr. Riley was in his room, reading by himself. Shannon said hello but he barely responded to his daughter.

Charley caught the look of sadness on Mr. Riley's face. He knew then that he and Shannon had done the right thing. Skip and his friends had to pay!

They sat down in the living room, switching on the television that Mr. Riley had bought Shannon for Christmas. Watching in a trance, they waited for the eleven o'clock news, holding their breaths. Sure enough, there was a story about two boys who had been shot in Port City. Rollie Danova and Peter McEvoy were found dead in their respective homes, both shot by the same gun. As yet, the police had no suspects, no clues as to who had ended the lives of the two Central Academy students.

"Wow," Charley muttered.

Shannon picked up the phone, dialing the Port City Police Department. "Hello? Yes, about the two boys who were shot. Andy Rothman did it. Yes, Andy Rothman. No, I don't want to tell you my name. Just check with Andy Rothman."

She hung up.

Charley looked at her. "What about Skip and Guy?"

"That's going to be a little more complicated," Shannon said. "If you don't want to help, you don't have to."

"In for a penny, in for a pound," Charley said. "That's what my father always says."

They sat there quietly, watching television, hoping for a special report.

But they'd have to wait until morning to hear the news.

It would be all over the papers, radio and television.

Andy Rothman was found in his room, dead from a self-inflicted gunshot wound.

The only words in his suicide note were, *I shot Rollie and Peter.*

The problem, for the most part, had taken care of itself.

SIXTEEN

The next Monday morning, Central Academy was abuzz with the bizarre news of the double murder and suicide. Everyone speculated as to the reason for Andy Rothman's strange behavior, but no one had the answer, not even Skip or Guy, the two remaining members of the gang. Police Chief Victor Danridge questioned many students, including Shannon and Charley, both of whom denied any knowledge of Andy's motives. By Monday afternoon, everyone had chalked it up to a mystery that would never be solved.

After the final bell, Shannon and Charley walked home in the cold air, saying very little. Shannon had occasional pangs of guilt, at least until she thought about her brother, sitting in his wheelchair in the hospital. Then the guilt went away, replaced by a weird feeling of satisfaction. Andy had evened the score for her, at least partially. The matter of Skip and Guy still remained.

"You okay?" Charley asked, his breath fogging the air.

She nodded. "I'm all right."

"I feel funny," Charley offered.

She turned to stare at him. "Are you sorry you helped me?"

He thought for a moment and then shook his head. "No. I'm not sorry. They had it coming. I just feel funny."

She sighed and started to walk again. "I feel funny too, but it isn't finished."

"Skip and Guy?"

"Yes, that's it. Skip and Guy."

"What are you going to do?" Charley asked.

She shrugged. "I don't know. I have to think about it. I have to study them."

And study them she did.

For the rest of the week, Shannon kept her eyes on Skip and Guy, watching, waiting for the answer to come to her.

Skip had an aura of relief about him, as if he were glad that his three friends were gone. Shannon caught him talking to Erin and several other girls in the hallway. Was he covering his bases? Making sure that his former victims were keeping their mouths shut? Shannon half-expected Skip to approach her, but he kept his distance, like he thought it wasn't necessary. Chief Danridge hadn't believed Shannon the first time around, so why would he believe her now?

Guy was a different story altogether. He slogged through the hallways, bombed out of his mind on something. He was totally out of it, lost in a stupor. He didn't even look at Shannon or anyone else for that matter.

It finally occurred to Shannon that Guy was the key to her final vengeance.

Guy was the weak link.

Shannon would have to use Guy if she wanted to get to Skip.

And she wanted to get to Skip in a big way.

Shannon sat in her living room, staring at the phone. Outside, a wind blew sheets of snow into the Tide Gate River. Ice floes were thick on the frozen surface of the water. Weather forecasters had been predicting record cold temperatures for Port City. But Shannon didn't care. She had been waiting for two weeks to try her new plan. It was time to make a move.

Charley sat on the couch next to her. He

had walked Shannon home from school that afternoon. It was Friday, February first, a day that would linger forever in Charley's thoughts.

"Are you going to do it?" he asked.

She nodded. "I have to start sometime. It might as well be now. Don't you think so?"

Charley looked away. "Man, I don't know what I think."

"Would you like to go with me to visit Patrick?"

He shook his head. "I don't think so."

Shannon picked up the phone. "Then we do it."

She dialed the number and listened for the voice on the other end. "Hello? May I speak to Guy?"

The words were slurred, but the voice was unmistakable. "This is Guy. Who's this?"

"It's Katie," she said in a lilting voice. "You remember me, don't you, Guy?"

He made a gurgling sound. "Katie? Are you out of the hospital? Are you all right?"

Click!

She hung up on him. "Wait a minute," she said to Charley.

Then she dialed the number again. "Guy? It's Katie. You know what you did to me."

"Katie, please. When did you get out of the loony bin? Huh? Can you come over?"

"You hurt me, Guy. You know you did."

"I'm sorry, Katie. I swear I didn't meant to hurt you. Please, come over. I want to see you. My parents went away for the weekend. We can talk about what happened."

"No, Guy. You have to live with what you did."

"Katie, I'm so sorry. I—"

Click!

Charley squinted at Shannon. "What did he say?"

"His parents are out of town for the weekend," Shannon replied. "He wants Katie to come over."

"So?"

Shannon smiled a little. "I think Katie should pay him a visit. Don't you?"

Charley wiped the sweat from his brow. "I don't know about this, Shannon."

"Do you know about my brother?" Shannon challenged. "Don't you remember what they did to him?"

Charley hung his head. "I—I don't want anyone else to die."

She sighed. "Neither do I. Maybe they won't have to die this time. Maybe we can get around it."

"How?"

"First things first," Shannon replied. "Now, tell me what Katie looked like. I want to be convincing."

With hesitation in his voice, Charley began to describe the girl who Skip had sent to the mental institution.

Guy's house was located in Prescott Estates, just a few blocks from Andy's place. When Shannon and Charley pulled up in the Lincoln, the windows were dark. Shannon peered toward the front door, wondering if Guy had gone out for the evening. What if he was on his way to Skip's house to tell him about the mysterious phone call from Katie? Skip would inform Guy that Katie was still in the mental institution.

"You think he's in there?" Charley asked.

Shannon let out a plaintive sigh. "I don't know. I think I have to go in to find out. How do I look?"

Charley studied Shannon's costume. The Central Academy cheerleading outfit belonged to Charley's older sister who had since gone on to college. Katie had been a cheerleader so it was the best way for Shannon to masquerade as the unfortunate victim of Skip's treachery.

"You look fine," Charley replied.

"Do I resemble Katie?"

Charley shrugged. "Yeah, I guess."

Shannon's hair, which was darker than Katie's, had been pushed under a red stocking cap.

"I hope Guy can't tell the difference," Shannon said.

Charley gazed at the house. "If he's in there, he's probably whacked out on his father's liquor."

Shannon opened the car door. "Here goes nothing."

"I'm right behind you," Charley replied.

Shannon looked back at him. "Where are you going?"

"I'm not letting you go in there alone, Shannon. Not with that fat idiot in there. You don't know what he's going to try."

Shannon nodded. "Okay, but stay out of the way."

"I promise I will."

They crossed the street, heading for the back door. Shannon's heart was throbbing, her arms and legs felt weak. This was the last phase of her scheme. If everything went as planned, Skip and Guy would both be sunk and no one would be hurt.

The back door was unlocked. Shannon entered the house and listened in the darkness. Charley stood behind her, holding his breath.

"I don't hear anything," he whispered.

Shannon moved forward, feeling her way through the shadows. When she reached the living room, she heard shallow breathing. She looked over her shoulder, waving for Charley to stop. He fell back into the kitchen, leaning against the wall.

Following the sound of the heavy rale, Shannon drew closer to a long, sectional sofa. Guy lay on the sofa, his mouth gaping open. A half-empty whiskey bottle sat on the coffee table next to the sofa. Shannon hoped that he wasn't too drunk. She had to wake him up if she was going to carry through with her plan.

"Guy?"

No response from the sofa.

She raised her voice. "Guy! Wake up!"

His head snapped forward and he sat up.

"Hello, Guy," Shannon said. "It's me, Katie."

His eyes squinted at her in the darkness. "Katie?"

"You dream about me, don't you, Guy? You have dreams about what you and the others did to me."

He nodded slowly. "Yes, I have dreams."

"You have to turn yourself in, Guy. You have to tell the police what you did. And you have to tell on Skip too. You have to make sure that he's punished."

His head began to roll around on his neck. "No. I can't."

"You must, Guy. Otherwise you'll have nightmares for the rest of your life. You'll never have another good night's sleep."

"No, Skip will kill me."

"The police will go easy on you if you confess, Guy. Skip will be the one in trouble."

"No, I—"

"Call the police, Guy, or I'll haunt you for the rest of your life. Do you hear me? The rest of your life."

Guy put his face in his hands and began to whimper.

Shannon receded into the shadows, joining Charley in the kitchen.

When Guy looked up, Katie was gone. "Katie! Katie, please come back."

Charley leaned closer to Shannon. "Let's get out of here," he whispered.

"No," Shannon replied. "I want to see if it worked. Listen, he's picking up the telephone. I knew it, he's going to call the police so he can tell them about Skip."

But when Guy's voice rose in the living room, it was singing an entirely different tune. "Skip. Yeah, it's me, Guy. Skip, it's Katie. She's been talking to me."

Shannon bit her lip. She had counted on

Guy calling the police. She never figured that he would turn to Skip.

"What?" Guy said into the receiver. "No, she isn't in the hospital. She's been calling me on the phone. She was just here. I swear it. Skip, listen—what? No, I'm all by myself. You want me to meet you. Where? Yeah, I can do that. You want me to leave now? Okay, I'm on the way. Yeah, I won't tell anyone. Okay, I'll see you there."

He hung up the phone and staggered to the door, grabbing his overcoat before he left.

"Damn," Shannon said.

"What are we going to do?" Charley asked.

"Follow him," Shannon replied.

"I'm not sure that's such a good idea."

Shannon wasn't sure either.

But they had to do it.

SEVENTEEN

The Lincoln moved slowly along River Street as they followed Guy in the falling snow. He staggered on the sidewalk, barely able to keep his balance. Where had Skip told Guy to meet him? They were almost on the banks of the river, near New Market. Why had Skip called his friend out here?

"Where the devil is he going?" Charley asked aloud.

"Just stay on him," Shannon replied. "I want to see what Skip has in mind."

She had a bad feeling in her stomach. Skip could be wickedly calculating. Guy might be in a lot of danger. Shannon didn't want to see Guy get hurt. Of the five boys who had accosted her, Guy seemed to be the only one with a conscience. Shannon would settle for seeing him go to the juvenile correctional institute to pay for his misdeeds.

Charley steered the Lincoln around a wide corner. The road started to slant upward. Suddenly the New Market Bridge loomed in front of them, dimly lighted in the falling snow.

"He's meeting Skip at the bridge," Shannon said.

Charley squinted through the drifting flakes of white. "The bridge? Why?"

Shannon grabbed the steering wheel. "Cut your lights and pull over. I think Skip is already here."

Charley guided the car to the curb and turned off the engine. "Can you see him?"

"No. We better get out."

"Shannon—"

"I don't want Guy to be hurt," she replied. "He didn't hurt me when he had the chance."

Charley shook his head. "I don't like this."

"Neither do I."

They climbed out of the Lincoln, trying to be quiet as they closed the door. Following Guy's footprints in the snow, they moved slowly toward the bridge. When Shannon saw Skip's Miata parked under a street lamp, she grabbed Charley and pulled him off the sidewalk. Both of them lost their balance, slipping on the ice, falling down an incline into a snowbank.

Charley raised his head. "What the—"

Shannon rolled over to face him. "I saw Skip. He's there. Come on, we have to get up."

After struggling for a few moments, they managed to crawl over the drift, only to tumble down the other side. Shannon picked herself up, dusting the snow from the red-and-white cheerleading uniform. Charley jumped to his feet next to her. They had landed at the edge of a small park where people sometimes picnicked in the summer.

"Over there," Shannon said, pointing to a stand of three evergreens. "Come on."

"Let's just call the police," Charley muttered.

"No!"

They stomped through the snow until they reached the green spruce branches that were laden with layers of white. Shannon peeked around the sagging boughs. She could see the dark images of Skip and Guy under the streetlight. They seemed to be talking in a friendly manner.

Charley bumped into her, peering over her shoulder. "What's going on?"

"Nothing. So far."

Suddenly, Skip began to wave his hands in the air. He pushed Guy. Guy fell into the snow. Skip stood over him, screaming in a voice that echoed down to Shannon and Charley.

Shannon started to move around the tree. "We have to help Guy. Come on."

Charley stopped her. "No, wait."

"Skip isn't that tough," she said. "It'll be three against one. If we—"

"What if Guy sides with Skip? Then it's two against two. You want to fight them straight up?"

Shannon hesitated. "No."

"So keep watching."

Charley had made his point. Shannon eased back behind the spruce tree. She continued to watch the two boys in the snow.

Skip seemed to calm down a little. He reached out, helping Guy to his feet. Guy swayed back and forth. He was still drunk. They talked for a few more minutes before Skip started to argue again.

This time, Guy tried to turn, to run away. Skip grabbed him by the collar of his overcoat, yanking him back. They both lost their balance, falling to the ground. They wrestled for a moment before Skip landed on top.

"He's going to hurt Guy," Shannon said.

Charley shook his head. "This is a hell of a time to start caring about Guy."

"I can't help it, Charley. When I was in that shack at the beach, Guy all but let me escape."

He sighed. "Okay, but let's watch for a little while longer. Maybe they won't—"

"Look! He's dragging Guy toward the bridge!"

Skip was on his feet now, pulling Guy over the snow. He was going to throw him into the frozen river. He was going to kill Guy so he wouldn't tell the police about Katie and the other girls.

She broke for the bridge, trying to catch them. Charley was right behind her. They tripped a couple of times, falling face down in the cold blanket of white.

We'll never catch them, she thought.

As she stood up, she peered toward the walkway that led up to the pedestrian crossing. Skip and Guy had disappeared in the shadows of the path. Shannon started to run again on leaden legs. The snow made it almost impossible. It was like the nightmare where her feet were plastered to the ground.

"Wait for me!" Charley called.

But she couldn't wait. If something happened to Guy, she'd regret it. He didn't deserve the same fate as the others.

When she reached the path that led up to the bridge, she stopped for a moment, trying to catch her breath. A scream from the pedestrian walkway prompted her forward. She didn't think about what she would do when she reached the struggling boys. She just wanted to get there.

"Shannon!" Charley cried. "Don't do it."

But she started to climb anyway. On the pedestrian walkway, she could feel the vibrations as Skip dragged Guy toward the middle of the bridge. Below them, the Tide Gate River was covered with a thick sheet of ice. There were breaks in the frozen surface and the icy river still flowed beneath them. Anyone falling from the bridge would never survive, even if the body fell in one of the open holes.

Skip's voice reached her in the falling snow. "That's it, fat boy," he said to Guy. "Come on, just a little bit further and you can go for a nice swim."

"No," Shannon whispered under her breath. "He can't."

She took a couple of steps toward them.

Skip stopped, trying to lift the heavy body. For a moment, Guy leaned against the railing. He reeled there as Skip bent down to grab his legs.

"Just a little bit more," Skip said. "Come on, you fat piece of crap. Get over the rail!"

Shannon was close to them now. "No!" she cried. "Don't do it, Skip!"

Skip stood up, gazing in her direction. His eyes grew wide. In the snow, he did not realize that it was Shannon.

Skip's jaw dropped. "Katie? Is that you?"

"Don't do it," Shannon repeated. "Please. Go to the police. Tell them what you did."

Skip laughed all of a sudden. "You aren't Katie!"

At that moment, Guy cried out and lunged for Skip. He caught Skip by the neck, wrapping his hands around Skip's throat. They began to struggle again.

"Stop it!" Shannon cried. "You're both going to fall!"

Charley ran up next to her, sucking cold air. "What the . . ."

"Stop them!" Shannon urged. "Please!"

Charley shook his head. "No way. If I go near them, they might throw *me* into the water."

"Charley—"

"Shannon, I can't!"

Skip lifted his foot, stomping Guy's ankle. A bone cracked in Guy's leg. He let go of Skip's throat. Skip knocked him to the walkway with a single punch. He stood over Guy, trying to catch his breath.

"Give it up, Skip," Charley said. "You

can't get away with it now. It's our word against yours."

Skip gazed at Charley with narrow eyes. His mouth opened to say something. But he never got the chance.

Guy stirred on the walkway, grabbing Skip's legs.

"No!" Skip cried.

Guy started to lift Skip from the walkway. Skip grabbed the rail, trying to hang on to the cold steel. But he couldn't keep his grip. And Guy managed to rise up, clinging tightly to Skip, lifting him over the rail.

"Don't!" Shannon cried. "Don't do it, Guy!"

But Guy didn't listen. He pushed Skip over the railing. Skip yelled all the way down, screaming one last time before his body slammed against the ice.

"No!" Shannon cried.

Guy turned to look at her. "I'm sorry, Katie. I'm sorry for what I did to you. For what we did to all of them."

Shannon ripped off the stocking cap. "I'm not Katie."

Guy looked down at the river. "I'm sorry, Katie. I'm so sorry for what I did. I have to pay."

"Damn it, I'm not Katie!"

Guy raised his injured leg, throwing it

on top of the rail. "I deserve this, Katie. I deserve to die."

Charley took a step toward him. "You idiot, she isn't Katie! She's Shannon!"

"Good-bye, Katie," Guy said softly. "I hope I see you in heaven. Please forgive me."

"Stop him, Charley!"

Guy started to roll over the railing.

Charley lunged for him, catching the sleeve of Guy's overcoat. For a moment, Guy dangled from Charley's grip. But he was simply too heavy for Charley to hold. Guy fell to the ice, landing next to Skip.

"My God," Charley muttered.

He gazed down at the bodies. They hung there for a moment on the sheet of ice. Then the ice cracked and they sank into the river, disappearing in the swift current.

Charley turned away from the spectacle, stepping toward Shannon. "We better get the police," he said.

Shannon grabbed his arm. "No, let's get out of here."

Charley squinted at her. "Shannon! They're dead. We have to tell Chief Danridge!"

She shook her head vehemently, tears forming in her eyes. "No! They'll find the bodies soon enough. And when they do, they'll talk to us. I want some time to recover, to get my head together. Besides, if Chief Danridge believed me in the first place, this never would've happened."

"Shannon—"

She stared into his eyes. "Charley, I love you. And if you love me, you won't say anything about this."

"You love me?" he said weakly.

Shannon nodded. "Yes, I do. Now come on. Let's get out of here before someone sees us."

Charley nodded. "Okay. You win." He took her hand.

They started back toward the Lincoln.

Shannon was right. The police would talk to them about what had happened to the two bodies that would turn up in the river. But she wouldn't say a word. She'd deny any knowledge of their fates, even when Chief Danridge challenged her.

Shannon would just keep thinking about her brother and what the five boys had done to him.

Even with that, she'd have a tough time trying to forget the horrid images that would forever haunt her dreams.

EPILOGUE

"Hey, Shannon!" Patrick cried. "Let's throw the Frisbee. Come on, hurry! It'll be dark soon."

Shannon smiled at her younger brother. He stood on a dark field of green grass and colorful wildflowers. She started to run after him, chasing him in the field.

"Hey, Shan! Look who's here!"

Shannon stopped, lifting her eyes to see the kind woman with her arms outstretched. "Mom!"

"It's Mom, Shannon. She's alive. And I'm not in the hospital anymore. Isn't it great?"

"Yeah," Shannon said. "Great."

Patrick waved to her. "Shannon, Mom wants to play Frisbee with us Isn't that rad?"

Shannon nodded, even though she knew

something was wrong. Her mother never liked to play Frisbee. She closed her eyes for a moment. And when she opened them, her mother and brother were gone.

"Hi, Shannon. Thrown anyone off a bridge lately?"

She took a step backward. "Skip!"

"I'm dead, Shannon. All because of you. Why don't you go turn yourself in to Chief Danridge? He knew you were lying when you told him you didn't know anything about my death."

She shook her head, whimpering. "No. It can't be. You're dead. You're all dead!"

Suddenly, the others appeared out of nowhere—Andy, Guy, Peter, and Rollie. They chased her through the field, nipping at her feet like wild dogs. Shannon managed to elude them as they chased her back to consciousness.

She sat up in her bed, staring at the bright casement of the window that opened onto the river. The dream always came right before she awakened. Her nightmare had different incarnations, but it was always the same field and the boys chasing her.

Climbing out of bed, Shannon went to the casement, throwing open the window. She gazed out onto the street on a sunny morning in May. It had been four months since Guy jumped from the New Market Bridge but the dream always brought back the memories. She drew in the salty air that wafted up from the Tide Gate River.

Shannon began to watch the street on this quiet Sunday. The bell tolled eight times in Market Square. Things had not been great in the last four months, but she had survived. Her father had stayed off the bottle and she had managed to pull a B average at Central Academy. Still, every day her life seemed to be burdened by a lead weight on her shoulders. She had begun to wonder if the dark veil would ever be lifted from her dreary existence.

When the Lincoln Town Car appeared on the street, Shannon found herself smiling. "Charley," she said to herself.

He pulled up next to the curb and got out of the car. He didn't see Shannon in the window so he started for the stairs. She stopped him by calling from above.

"Hey, handsome."

Charley glanced up, grinning. "You're up early for a Sunday."

"I had some weird dreams."

He had been so good to her, sticking with her during the past few months of misery. On the bridge, she had said she loved him to keep him from going to the police. But now she knew she had spoken the truth.

Shannon loved Charley with all her heart—what was left of it anyway.

"I thought I'd drive you out to see Patrick," he told her. "Dad let me have the car."

"I'll be right down."

She dressed quickly, rushing into the living room to find her father asleep on the couch. "Dad? Wake up."

Mr. Riley opened his eyes. "Morning. I guess I fell asleep in front of the television."

Her father had been doing fairly well in light of the circumstances. He was even going out with a woman he had met at work. Mr. Riley didn't go to see Patrick as much anymore. It was too tough for him to look at his son in the wheelchair, drooling like an imbecile.

"I'm heading out with Charley," she told him. "Are you going to be all right?"

He nodded, wiping the sleep from his eyes. "Yeah. Jeanette and I are going over to Kittery today to shop at the outlets. I'll be okay. Will you be home for dinner tonight?"

"I'll call you," she replied, giving him a peck on the cheek. "See you later, Dad. Have a good day."

The sun was shining brightly as she emerged from the stairwell. She embraced

Charley, kissing him on the lips. He drew back, gawking at her.

"What's wrong?" she asked.

Charley laughed a little. "You haven't kissed me like that before."

"Didn't you like it?"

"Yeah, I loved it. Come on, I'll take you to the hospital."

Shannon grabbed his arm. "Charley, I don't want to go to the hospital today."

"You don't?"

She shook her head. "No, I want to go somewhere nice. Didn't you say your father has a cabin at Thunder Lake?"

"Uh, sure. You want to go out there?"

"Yes, I do."

Charley opened the door for her. "Then let's do it."

Shannon leaned back in the front seat as they drove away from Port City. She had decided to follow in her father's footsteps. She was never going back to the hospital to see Patrick. What good would it do? Her younger brother didn't know her anymore. He was gone.

Shannon had to start trying to let go of the pain.

She had to live again.

She had to put the darkness behind her once and for all.

Don't miss
WHISPERS FROM THE GRAVE

The similarities between Jenna and Rita were uncanny. They looked and acted exactly alike. Each was experiencing the thrill of first love. Each was empowered with a gift of the supernatural. And each harbored dark secrets. Jenna and Rita could have been sisters. Except for one thing . . .

Rita was murdered over a century ago.

———————

*Keep reading for a special sneak preview
of this exciting new suspense novel
by Leslie Rule!*

Sometimes I wished I'd never found Rita's diary. If I'd known all the trouble it would cause, I would have left it in its hiding place. But how could I have known that little musty book with its yellowing pages and rusty keyhole would get me involved in a murder?

My neighbor, Suki, was with me when I found the diary. We were poking around the attic of my family's old, rambling house.

It was built way back in 1870 and was actually made from real wood. That's rare here on Puget Sound. The old blind man who lived across the street said they stopped using wood to build houses around 2035 because of the tree shortage.

Suki's house was made from fiberglass and never needed to be painted like our funky old house did.

"Ick! A spider!" Suki suddenly shrieked. It skittered across the dusty floor on its thick, feathery legs and disappeared into a crack in the attic wall.

"It won't hurt you," I said. "We're used to spiders here. This house isn't airtight like yours. There are lots of places for bugs to get in."

She shuddered, her shoulders rising so they touched the ends of her limp blond hair. "Let's go back downstairs to your room where there aren't as many bugs."

"Go ahead," I said and was relieved when she didn't. Last time she was alone in my room, I think she filched my new tube of strawberry lip tinter.

Suki had acted like my shadow ever since we moved to Banbury Bay in July when Mom inherited Great-aunt Ashley's old house. Just because Suki lived down the beach from us, and my father worked with her uncle at Twin-Star Labs, she acted as if we should be automatic best friends. I don't mean to sound cruel, but I preferred not to spend so much time with her. Suki was clingy and insecure, and she scared all the boys away with her mousey ways.

If she didn't stop hanging around me, I'd never fit in at Banbury High. At my old school in Salem, Oregon, I'd always been kind of an outsider.

I was branded a rebel in the second grade—all because of a misunderstanding on a rainy afternoon. The stigma stayed with me forever. Or at least until we moved to Banbury Bay.

Sometimes when I looked back on that strange day in Salem, I got goose bumps. I couldn't explain what happened, and all these years later I still wondered. *I don't want to think about that.* That is behind me now.

I saw our move to Banbury Bay as a chance to start a new life, with new friends. But I knew I couldn't spend every waking moment with Suki unless I wanted to be labeled a total spard. It's a hard, cold fact that the crowd you hang with influences how people view you.

"This old house of yours really gives me the creeps, Jenna," Suki said. "Your attic is probably full of rats. Let's get out of here!"

"No, I want to see what's in this old trunk," I said, pulling a rusty bicycle off the dust-coated trunk in the corner.

"Probably more spiders."

I ignored her and popped open the lid. A thick, musty odor nearly knocked me over.

"It's just a bunch of old clothes," she said, peering over my shoulder.

It didn't look like anything too exciting. They were mostly faded blue jeans and ragged T-shirts. But I dug through the pile, partly because I was hoping Suki would get tired of watching me and leave my house. "Look at this!" I said, "It's a pair of old overalls. Somebody embroidered little hearts and peace signs on them. Do you think they belonged to a farmer?"

"There's something sticking out of the pocket!"

It was an old diary. A *very* old diary—its secrets long ago locked between the fading red vinyl cover. It would be easy to pick the lock. Someone had scribbled PRIVATE across the cover. For an instant, I considered tucking it back in the overalls. After all, what right did I have to read a stranger's secrets?

"Who did it belong to?" Suki's pale blue eyes sparkled with sudden interest.

"Whoever it was is probably dead," I said. *Do the dead have a right to privacy?* I wondered. I turned the little book over and set it on the floor. "I could pick the lock if I had a piece of wire." The words were barely out of my mouth when the lock suddenly popped open—all by itself.

"Weird!" Suki whispered. "Maybe you've got ghosts up here!"

A shiver ran through me, but I laughed it off. "Would you relax? The lock was just worn out. I must have jostled it when I set it down, and it broke. That's all."

I opened the diary and a black and white photograph fluttered out. I stared into the familiar face and gasped.

"That's you!" Suki said. "How did a picture of

you get in that old diary? And who is that *cute* guy next to you?"

I couldn't answer her. All I could do was stare at the girl in the photograph. She had *my* face! The wide spaced eyes. The button nose sprinkled with freckles. The slight overbite and too thin lips. Those were *my* features. But it wasn't a picture of me. I was certain.

I turned over the photograph and read: *Rita and Ben, Stones concert, Seattle Coliseum, 1970*. That picture was a *hundred* years old!

I finally found my voice. "It's not me. This picture was taken a century ago."

"She sure looks like you. She's even built like you, Jenna."

It was true. Rita had my long (but too skinny) legs and slim waist. She wore a flowered halter top and a faded pair of cut-off jeans embroidered with peace signs. Had Rita embroidered the overalls too? They must have been hers, I realized.

"Maybe that's you in another life," Suki suggested. "Maybe you were reincarnated."

"She's probably a relative of mine. We have the same genes. It's natural I'd inherit some of my family's characteristics," I said, trying to make sense of the eerie resemblance.

"It's not like she's your mom or something for Pete's sake! She's a *distant* relative. If she was really born a hundred years ago, the genes would be watered down by now. You could inherit her nose or something, but not her *whole* face!"

Suki was right. It didn't make sense I would look so much like a relative who was born a century before me. The fact is, I don't even resemble anyone in my immediate family. My parents are both short and round, while I am long and slender. I don't have my dad's prominent nose or my mom's startling violet eyes. My nose is one of those tiny, upturned models and my eyes are an uninteresting gray. I'm different from my parents in so many ways, I can't even count them. I thought about this as I walked Suki home.

Her house is about a quarter of a mile from us. It's right on the water—so close the waves swish against her dining room window when it storms. When we arrived, Suki scurried inside and I leaned on the railing of the Gradys' deck and stared at the horizon. The sunset had deepened to purple, and the beach was cloaked in shadows. Suki's father, Dr. Grady, poked his head out the door. "It's getting dark. I'll drive you home," he said, his scraggly eyebrows drawing together in concern.

I waved him away. "I walk fast. I'll be home before it's completely dark. Tell Suki I'll phone her," I called over my shoulder.

I lied to Dr. Grady. I had no intention of walking fast. I strolled slowly, inhaling the pungent, salty air and savoring the peaceful moments alone. The only sound was the gentle slapping of the waves. It felt good to get away from Suki's constant chatter.

Halfway home, my finger-watch phone beeped. Suki's face—in 3-D—appeared on my watch face. *Now what does she want?*

"Jenna, are you there?" Suki called. "Can you hear me?"

For a moment, I felt as if a miniature Suki face was growing from my finger, like an annoying planter's wart that refused to fall off. I turned off the finger-phone and her image vanished. Then I settled in on one of the huge logs a storm had washed ashore and opened Rita's diary, which I had carried with me from home. The light had nearly faded away so I read by my keyring flash-light.

March 3, 1970

Dear Diary,

I never should have listened to April! She told me I should "Play hard to get!" She said Ben would lose interest if I didn't "Act aloof" once in a while. She said—AND I QUOTE—"Men like a little mystery."

Well, I took April's advice. And I'd give anything if I hadn't. While I was busy being aloof, some tramp got her claws into the love of my life!

Why did I listen to April? She's never even had a boyfriend and has only been on three dates, and they were only with that skinny guy who bags groceries—Marvin Fudsomething-or-other. Does that make her an expert????? I think not!

Maybe April WANTED to break me and Ben up because Shane doesn't want to date her. (Shane Murdock is Ben's best friend and he's gorgeous—though not as gorgeous as Ben.)

I guess I shouldn't be mad at April, but I have to blame someone. It hurts so bad. For the first time in my life, I'm really in love. I know I've said it before, but it was NEVER like this. Oh, Diary, I know I haven't told you anything about Ben. And I know I promised to write my every thought in you. But I've been so busy since I met him, I haven't had time. Now, as my tears fall on your pages, smearing the ink, I'll try to fill you in on the last weeks.

Diary, it started with his eyes. Ben had these really far-out eyes. They're the same shade of blue as a faded pair of jeans. And when he looks at me, I feel like he's looking into my soul. I know that sounds corny but—oh! Someone's knocking at the door. Maybe it's Ben!

I'm back, Diary. It wasn't Ben. No one was at the door. That's kind of scary, because I'm here alone. Mom's at her yoga class and Dad's giving a guitar lesson. Jim is probably out raising hell on his bicycle with all the other 11-year-old brats in the neighborhood. So when I answered the door and didn't see anybody, I slammed it fast. I kind of had the feeling someone was hiding in the bushes! I went around the house and locked all the windows, just in case. Lately I've had this really weird feeling that someone's watching me!

A sudden sharp crack interrupted Rita's words. I nearly dropped the diary as I turned quickly toward the noise. It sounded like a twig snapping under a foot. But I couldn't see anyone. Immersed in Rita's world, I hadn't noticed the night creep in. The logs were shapeless shadows blending with the beach, and the water had turned black.

"Who is it? Who's there?" I called out tentatively. "Suki, is that you?" It wouldn't be exactly like her to follow me home when I'd just gotten rid of her. The pest!

Only the waves answered me, their rhythmic whispers caressing the sand. I aimed my flashlight in the direction the noise had come from—or rather where it seemed to come from. On the water sound plays tricks. No one was there.

I stuffed the diary back into my pocket and headed toward home, this time walking briskly.

The distinct sound of footsteps crunching on rocks came behind me. *Someone is following me!*

My heartbeat thudded in my ears as I began to run. I bounced forward and my feet slid across the slippery, seaweed-coated rocks. Stumbling, I fell to my knees. Barnacles sharp as razors scraped the palms of my hands as I scrambled to my feet.

Adrenaline coursed through me, fueling me

with a surge of energy that kept my legs pumping.
I nearly flew over the beach, kicking unseen
sticks and sea whips out of my path, running for
my life.

I rounded the bend and was greeted by a
ferocious bark. Relief flooded through me. It was
old Mr. Edwards and his seeing-eye dog, Jake.

"Who's there?" Mr. Edwards yelled.

I skidded to a stop, gasping for breath. "It's me,
Mr. Edwards! It's Jenna. Someone was following
me!"

"Don't worry. Jake will take care of them," he
said. "You can walk with us. We wander down
here every night so Jake can do his business. That
way I don't have to clean up after him. The tide
comes in and does it for me."

"Sounds like a good system," I said politely.

"May I give you a piece of advice, young lady?"

"Sure."

"Don't walk on the beach alone after dark
anymore. It's not safe for you. Did you know a girl
was murdered here?"